THE TRAIL TO REDEMPTION

PLAINSMAN WESTERN SERIES BOOK ONE

B.N. RUNDELL

WOLFPACK
PUBLISHING
— EST 2013 —

The Trail to Redemption
Print Edition
© Copyright 2021 B.N. Rundell

Wolfpack Publishing
5130 S. Fort Apache Rd. 215-380
Las Vegas, NV 89148

wolfpackpublishing.com

Paperback ISBN 978-1-63977-000-7
eBook ISBN 978-1-63977-001-4
LCCN 2021950205

THE TRAIL TO REDEMPTION

There are so many that are involved in producing the book you hold in your hands. The author is but one cog in the wheel because once the author is done scribbling, then the real work begins. The editors, proofreaders, cover designers, marketers, and so many more. Of course, that entire crew comes under the direction of Mike Bray at Wolfpack Publishing. And it was Mike who gave me the opportunity to put words to paper and eventually see those words literally circumnavigate the globe. So, thanks to Mike Bray, Rachel Del Grosso, Lauren Bridges, and the many others that compose his amazing staff at Wolfpack! You're the best!

He pushed the blackened timber with his toe, charcoal dust rising as it moved; he was looking around the remains of the barn and tack shed. He choked on the dust, coughed and spat, and lifted his neckerchief to cover his mouth and nose. Dust had settled round about, weeds were growing up through the debris, two fence posts still stood, naked of any cross-bars. He turned back toward the remains of the house, although little was left of his childhood home. What had been his mother's pride and joy, the rose garden on either side of the front porch, was overgrown and bore but one bud of a red rose. The pile of blackened timbers and ashes held little resemblance to his harbored memories. He dropped his eyes, shuffling his feet as he walked around the place. He looked behind the house at the tall maple where he and his brothers often climbed to escape their little sister. He heard her fussing below, wanting to join them, and saw her turn away and dejectedly walk to the house. One frayed rope hung from the big branch where a swing had been his sister's favorite pastime and he could hear her giggle and laugh as he pushed her higher.

Nestled between the oaks was the family plot and Reuben Grundy, the 19-year-old veteran of several battles in the service of Berdan's Sharpshooters, trudged toward the low fence and the markers, his green wool uniform britches gathering dust and stickers. He shook his head, glanced around, and moved closer. Three carved wooden headboards stood side by side, all with the same date. *Micah Grundy, 1801-1862, Rachel Grundy, 1812-1862, Rephael Grundy, 1846-1862.* Tears filled his eyes and made muddy rivulets down his cheeks. He wiped at his face with his sleeve, snot trailing down the sleeve and smearing the dust of the trail. He shook his head, remembering just two months past lying in the field hospital beside his brother, Rufus. Both had taken bullets in the assault at the Battle of Malvern Hill, what had been the final fight of the Seven Days Battles in Virginia. His brother had taken two bullets to the chest and bits of a grape shot from the artillery that tore up his neck and shoulder. As Reuben sat at bedside, Rufus squeezed his hand and made him promise to take care of the family, "You've gotta do it, brother. You're the oldest now and they need you!" he muttered, forced a smile, closed his eyes, and breathed his last. Now, his older brother lay buried in a military cemetery somewhere in Virginia, leaving an empty space in the family plot. He hung his head, remembering his mother, the red head who had caught his father's eye when she rode into the little village of White Pigeon, Michigan territory. There was not much there but she was bound and determined to start a school. They were married soon after and the only school she started was in the home that now lay in ashes. The oldest boy, Rufus, a biblical name meaning

2

red haired, came along soon after, followed by Reuben and Rephael and finally the only daughter, who bore the same name as their mother, Rachel, and looked just like her.

Reuben and Rephael favored their father, who was the spitting image of his Swedish mother with a big build, light complexion, and thick blonde hair. When Reuben was quick to join up after the attack on Fort Sumter, his older brother soon followed, but Rephael was encouraged to stay home and help with the family farm. Rachel, only a year younger than the youngest boy, was betrothed to the neighbor, George Hanover, and was wed shortly after the brothers left. Now, he stood looking around what had been the family farm; from what he could tell, this destruction and killing had happened early summer. The crops had been planted but left untended and now were wasting in the fields. The fall colors were showing in the hardwood forests that surrounded the farm and Reuben guessed it to be mid-September.

He sat down on the little bench beside the graves and began talking to his departed family, "So, what do I do now, Pa? You know I was never one that took to the farming, that was Rufus and Rephael more'n me. And how do I find out who did this?" he shrugged as he looked around; it had been too long since it happened for any sign to remain. Everything had been destroyed or stolen. The barn had been stripped of tack and gear before it burned, the animals were gone, nothing remained of the house. But everything he looked at brought memories flooding back. Memories of his youth, fishing in the creek, running barefoot through the fields, riding Meg, the mule, and the days spent on the porch doing the schoolwork their Ma demanded. Then

3

he remembered, his Pa had always had his 'rainy day fund' set aside. He stood, turning back toward the remains of the house and the well that stood between the barn and the home. It had been caved in, the stone base crumbled, the rope, pulley and bucket gone, but Reuben walked closer. He looked around, concerned about being seen, then dropped to one knee beside the stones. With his calloused fingers, he dug at the edge of a flat stone that was where they would stand to turn the crank to raise and lower the bucket. He pried it up and saw what he hoped for, the metal box Pa had used as his 'only trustworthy bank.'

With another glance around, he wiped off the box, pried open the lid and was surprised at the contents. At one side was a draw-string leather pouch but lying loose in the bottom were several coins. He lifted the pouch, hefted its weight, and pulled it open. He had already guessed the contents were coins but these were still shiny gold double eagles. A folded note showed his father's handwriting, "Rufus Bounty." It was the money paid to late enlistees for enlisting in the Union Army. Rufus had received a thousand dollars from a combination of local, state, and federal bounties, and had his father keep it for him or use it if necessary. As he fingered the other coin, he guessed there was at least that much, perhaps more, in the loose coin. He lifted out the box, replaced the stone, and walked back to the graveside.

He sat the box between his feet in the tall grass, gave a heavy sigh, "So, this is a lot of money, Pa. I'm thinkin' I need to go into town, see Rachel and George, and try to find out who did this. If they haven't been caught already, maybe I should be doin' that." He paused, looking at the headstones, "Yeah, I know Ma, 'Vengeance is mine, saith the Lord.' That's what you'd say, but . . ." he shook his head. He was tired of killing. He had been a corporal in the Sharpshooters and had worked alone. He had repeatedly been sent out to delay the Confederates in their attacks and delay meant to kill as many officers and others as possible. It started with the Battle of Williamsburg, then Hanover Court House, then the Seven Days battles. Every time he pulled the trigger on his Sharps, somebody died. He never missed and some of his shots were over five hundred yards. At the last battle, his telescopic sight was on a colonel but just as he pulled the trigger, the officer's horse reared up and took the bullet, but the colonel broke his neck in the fall.

Reuben touched the scars on his chest where he had taken two bullets just below his collar bone, at the tail end of the last battle, and woke up in the field hospital next to his brother. His twelve-month enlistment was up but, with his wounds, he would have been sent home anyway, if for nothing else but recuperation. He never expected to come home to this, he thought as he looked around again. He had collected his back pay and had enough to buy a mule and tack when he got off the train at Elkhart. He still had his army-issued Sharps rifle, his Remington Army revolver, and his big Bowie knife. He wore the dark green britches of his uniform but had replaced the shirt with a green wool plaid. His army-issue frock coat, also in the dark green of the sharp-shooters, lay across the McClellan saddle.

The mule stood hipshot in the shade of the oak trees as Reuben rose and went to his side. With another glance around, he dumped the loose coin in one side of the saddlebags atop his loosely folded spare shirt and other sundries. The coin pouch was placed in the other side and he stuffed the small frying pan and extra ammunition on top. He touched his pistol where it rested at an angle on his left hip, butt forward, a position he favored from the many times he climbed into trees or atop rocky promontories to take his shots as a sharpshooter. His Bowie knife was in a sheath behind his belt, also at an easily accessible angle, at the small of his back. Out of necessity, he had become exceptionally proficient with all his weapons for, as a solitary sharpshooter, he had no one to rely on to watch his back or to help him in a fight and, often, he had to take on more than one and do it as silently as possible, for he was usually behind enemy lines.

With the mule in tow, he walked back to the graves, looked from one to the other, "Pa, Ma, Rephael, I might not be back. I'm gonna see if I can find who done this but, first, I'm gonna call on Rachel, let her know I'm home but soon to be gone. Ma, I know I promised you I'd do my best to walk with the Lord but where I've been and where I'm goin', I don't think the Lord has been. And Pa, like you always said, I'll do my best." He replaced his hat, swung aboard the tall mule, and started through the woods, taking the back trail to the neighbor's farm, where he hoped to find his sister, Rachel.

He stopped beside the creek and stepped down as the big mule dipped his nose in the gurgling water for a long drink. Reuben went to one knee and scooped up a handful to wash his hands and face, he loosened his collar and scrubbed his neck and upper chest, quickly dipped his head in the creek and slung his head back to rid the thick blonde hair of most of the water. He winced at the pain from his wound but it was healing nicely and this was the most refreshed he felt since boarding the train. He mounted up and pushed through the brush and trees to come into the open near the remains of the neighbor's house and barn. It too, had been burnt to the ground. His heart sunk as he thought of his sister and slowly nudged the mule toward the debris.

He rode around the homesite, looking for the family plot, the tall grasses browning at the tips and waving in the low breeze. He finally spotted the plot set back in the edge of trees. He stepped down, removed his hat, and walked slowly toward the low picket fence. His eyes fell on the tallest of the monuments, a carved sandstone marker with letters worn and faded. This was the stone of the patriarch of the Hanover clan, Ephraim. Beside his was a smaller stone that marked the grave of his wife, Ruth, another for an infant son. Two markers told of Ezekiel and Miriam, George's parents, and the dates showed they passed in '60 and '61. Reuben remembered the funeral for Miriam but he was gone to war when Ezekiel died. No other markers showed recent burials and Reuben breathed a deep sigh of relief.

He turned to the mule, "Well, Rufus, guess we need to go into town, find out about my sister, Rachel!" He chuckled at his calling the mule after his older brother; it just seemed to fit, since Rufus had often been called, 'stubborn as a mule'. He swung aboard and sighted between the tall ears for White Pigeon.

I t was a rickety bridge that crossed the White Pigeon river, the mule's hooves clattering with every step. It reminded Reuben of the drummer that foretold of the march or attack of the soldiers and now his approach was similarly announced. There was not much to the town, a general store, post office, land office, haberdashery, tavern, café, and a marshal's office. A handful of houses stood in line behind the business street and a livery stood alone at the far end. Reuben was reminded of the story his Pa told, about the early days of the settlement. This was all the land of the Potawatomi Indians but they were friendly with the white settlers. When there was a gathering of chiefs in the Detroit area, the chief, *Wahbememe,* which means White Pigeon, learned of plans to attack the settlement. The chief did not want his friends harmed and he set out to warn them, traveling by foot, running most of the way, the one-hundred-fifty miles to the settlement to warn the people. He gave the warning, collapsed, and died of exhaustion. The settlers named the town after the chief.

Reuben started up the dusty street, glancing at each of the structures and the few people that walked the boardwalk and two men who sat on rickety chairs leaning back against the weathered clapboard of the general store. A rooster raced across the street, barely outdistancing a hound dog in hot pursuit. Reuben chuckled, nudged the mule toward the marshal's office, reined up and stepped down to tether Rufus at the hitchrail.

He stretched his long leg up to the boardwalk, stood tall and hoisted his britches up and tucked in his shirt and stepped through the open door. He paused, squinting in the dim light, but quickly noticed the room was empty, jail doors stood open and papers on the desk fluttered in the draft. Reuben turned back to the board-walk, glanced at the mule, and strode up the walk to the general store. As he passed the loafers, they nodded as did he then he glanced in the window. Seeing no one, he stepped through the doorway, hearing a small bell over-head ring as he pushed open the door. With a chuckle, he pushed the hat to the back of his head and stepped into the waft of smells and colors. He paused, looking around at the stuffed shelves, stacked good, a big pickle barrel, and at the back, a counter with a smiling woman busy at her work.

"Reuben!" The sound of his name coming from an aproned clerk behind the counter startled him and he frowned to look her direction. His expression relaxed as he watched the young woman scurry from behind the counter, a broad smile splitting her face and tears dancing in her eyes as she hurried toward him. He recognized the dimpled face of his little sister, Rachel, as he opened wide his arms to catch her as she jumped at him, her arms reaching for his neck. She hugged him tightly, rubbing her cheek against his and he felt the warm tears course between them. She leaned back to look at him, barely able to distinguish his features through her tears. What she saw was a hardened lifeless stare, spider lines at the edge of his eyes and frown lines at his cheeks. Weathered skin contrasted with the dark blonde hair, but strength and resolve painted his countenance.

His hands at her waist, he pushed her back for a good look and he saw not just his sister, but his mother as well. Relief and happiness pushed its way to her expression as she slowly shook her head. She smiled and lay her head on his chest as she whispered, "You saw?"

He slowly nodded but held her close. As she calmed, she pushed back and asked, "Rufus?" and tears filled her eyes again as Reuben dropped his eyes and shook his head.

"He died in my arms after the last battle. We were together in the field hospital."

She frowned, "Together? You were wounded too?" she asked, frowning and looking him over for any sign of a wound.

"We were both hit near the end of the fight. He took a couple of bullets too but he also got hit with some grape shot. That's what done him in. But . . . we were together at the last."

"But you, are you alright?"

"Yeah, but I need to know what happened."

Movement at the curtain that separated the back room from the store front caught their attention and when a man pushed through, Rachel said, "George! Look who's here!"

"Reuben?" questioned a man with a receding hairline over a furrowed brow, thick eyebrows and spectacles that clouded his pale blue eyes. Sunken cheeks and a long neck reminded Reuben of the nickname, Goose, the brothers had hung on the man of their sister's fancy. He had a gingham shirt, sleeve garters, a long tan apron, and corded britches. He stepped forward, smiling, and extending his hand to shake with his brother-in-law. They clasped hands, slapped each other on the shoulder and laughed. "You'll stay for supper?"

Reuben ducked his head, nodding, then looked at George and to Rachel, "But, I need to know what happened. Thought I'd check with the marshal." He paused, looked back at George, "Do you know who?"

George glanced nervously to Rachel and back to Reuben, "Yes, but we don't know who all was involved. They called themselves the Home Guard and struck out at anybody who didn't do what they were told. Our place was empty when they hit it but yours, well, word was that your Pa had been hoarding and hiding gold coin for years, least that was the rumor since, well, long before you left. So, folks think they were after his stash and he wouldn't give it, so. . ."

He shrugged as he shook his head.

"They just killed all three of 'em? And nothin's been done?"

Rachel reached to touch Reuben's arm and shook her head, "No, no. Rephael was killed before that. Near as we can tell, he was hunting in the woods and came across a squad of Union soldiers. They thought he was a Confederate and was shooting at them. They caught him, tied him, and hung him. Pa found him the next day with a sign on him, 'This is what happens to johnny rebs!'"

The thought that soldiers of his own stripe had killed his brother brought up bile and choked him as he shook his head, picturing the soldiers striking down his brother. Yet he knew any soldiers stationed here in Michigan would either be trainees or rejects from the front lines and there would be no way of determining who or even when they were here. He shook his head again as he gritted his teeth and snarled, "But the Home Guard killed Ma and Pa?"

Rachel nodded, "We'll talk more at supper. Put up your horse in the barn behind the house," she pointed to the rear of the store, "George'll close up here and I'll come with you to the house."

Reuben glanced around, nodded, and watched as Rachel stripped off her apron, and frowned. She saw his expression and placed her hands on her swollen midriff and smiled, "Yes, you're going to be an uncle!" and giggled at his surprise. They walked together on the boardwalk; her hand tucked in the crook of his elbow as she leaned her head against his shoulder. He stood head and shoulders above the petite redhead and she delighted in walking at his side. When they neared the marshal's office, he said, "I think I'll ask the Marshal a thing or two. If you want to go to the house, I'll come along soon."

"Or I can stay at your side and make sure you come!" snickered Rachel as she smiled up at her brother.

"Or you can stay by my side," replied a smiling Reuben. They stepped to the open doorway, Rachel walked through followed closely by Reuben, as they were hailed and greeted, "Howdy stranger! Oh, it's you, Rachel. What can I do you fer?" Reuben stopped, squinted for his eyes to adjust to the dim interior, and spotted a man leaning back in a chair behind a makeshift desk with his feet propped up on the desk and his hands clasped behind his head. A marshal's badge hung loosely to the pocket that was stuffed with a Durham tobacco pouch, the tag hanging beside the badge.

"Marshal Montgomery, this is my brother, Reuben. He's just back from the war and has some questions for you."

The man scowled, dropped his feet to the floor and leaned forward, elbows on the desk and looked at Reuben, "What side you fit with?"

"The Union."

"You ain't wearin' blue." He snarled as he leaned to the side to look at Reuben's attire, "What color's that, green?"

"That's right. But what does the color of my clothes have to do with anything? Or do you expect everybody to dress in, what," he frowned as he made a show of looking at the attire of the marshal, "dirty brown and tobacco stains?"

The man snarled and jumped to his feet, leaned forward against his desk to reach for Reuben who stepped back out of reach. "Now watch your mouth, young'un! Sides, how'm I s'posed to know what outfit you be with since you ain't got no uniform! This here's Union territory and we don't abide no Johnny Rebs!"

Reuben let a slow grin cross his face, "So, what do you do, sic the Home Guard on 'em?"

The man was full of bluff and bluster and started to retort but was stopped by the calm and quiet voice of Rachel, "Now boys, we're all on the same side here," as she stepped between the men. Reuben looked down at his sister, up at the dirty-faced marshal and nodded as he stepped back.

"Now, what's your questions?" growled the scruffy-looking man as he plopped down on his chair.

"What's been done about the so-called Home Guard that murdered my folks and burnt their farm?"

The Marshal shook his head, leaned forward, "Now, I'm almighty sorry about that but them what done it left town right after and we ain't seen 'em since. I couldn't go after 'em, had to stay here and mind the town, what with the war an' all."

Rachel spoke again, "But Marshal, isn't he," nodding to a lone man in one of the cells, the only one with the door now closed, "one of them?"

The marshal leaned back and looked at the young man stretched out on the cot in the cell, "Yeah, he was. But he wasn't there when they hit your folks place. He left 'em 'fore that. When they hit the Hightower place, he said he wasn't havin' none of what they were doin' and he left 'em. That's why the judge just gave him six months and he's been workin' that off, what with sweepin' the boardwalk and such."

"Has he told you anything about what the others were planning?" asked Reuben.

"Ain't said nuthin'," replied Montgomery.

"So no one has any idea where they went?"

The marshal just shook his head in response.

"What about who they were?"

"Dunno."

Reuben scowled at the marshal, glanced to Rachel, then turned away, motioning his sister to come, and the two left the office. Reuben was visibly upset but slipped the reins free of the hitchrail and looked to Rachel to lead the way home. She looked at the mule, "That's not a horse!" she declared, giggling.

Reuben laughed, "Don't make fun of Rufus!"

"Rufus?! You named your mule after your brother?" she asked, incredulous.

"Doesn't it fit?"

She giggled as she nodded and motioned him to follow her around the back of the marshal's office toward her home.

"I don't think he even went out to the farm to see what was done," declared Rachel. They were seated around the table, the supper dishes stacked on the counter by the sink, and they savored the moment with hot cups of coffee.

"Has he done anything?" asked Reuben, glancing from George to Rachel. They were discussing the inability of the town marshal to apprehend those guilty of the atrocities in the community under the name of the Home Guard.

"Some have suspected he was a part of the Guard," mumbled George, adjusting the corner of the gingham tablecloth.

"But we don't know that," added Rachel, giving her husband a raised eyebrow with her glare.

"What about the one in jail? You said he had been a part of the bunch. Surely he knows their names and maybe even their plans, wouldn't he?" asked Reuben, glancing from Rachel to George. He had begun to notice that the stronger member of this marriage was his little sister but, as he recalled, George had never been a strong personality type. He looked back at his sister, waiting for her reply.

"There had been talk among the townsfolk that the marshal had protected him and kept that information to himself."

"Did he say, the man, what's his name?" he started, frowning.

"Jesse, Jesse Towns. His family were dirt farmers over near Niles until his father left them. Jesse tried to join up but he had the consumption and couldn't breathe well. After so many signed up, the only ones left were the felons, rejects, and cowards."

"I resent that! I paid three hundred dollars for my exemption!" huffed George. "I had sold the family farm and wanted to start our business, the general store, but I couldn't do that and go to war! The people of the community needed the store for supplies and more and I could not in good conscience leave my new bride!"

With a smile and a touch to his hand, Rachel said, "Sweetheart, no one is blaming you. We agreed it was best. But I'm talking about those that became the outlaws and ruffians and called themselves the Home Guard." She turned back to Reuben, "We suspected some of the ne'er do wells that hung around the tavern but nothing was done. After the farm burned, the entire bunch just disappeared. The only family that remains is the McNulty family but the father's a drunk and the mother, well . . ."

Reuben frowned, looked at George, "You said you sold the farm, who to?"

"The banker over in Niles. He comes to town ever so often, looks to do his banking business about town, and often buys and sells property. Why? You want to sell your farm?"

"I thought about it but it's as much Rachel's as mine."

"No, Reuben. That farm was always meant for you boys." She reached over to put her hand on George's and smiled at him. As she turned back to Reuben, "If you want to sell it, I'm guessing you want to go somewhere away from the war and get a new start. Is that right?"

He dropped his eyes, slowly shaking his head, "I don't think there's anywhere on this earth that I can go to get far enough away from the war." His eyes glazed over as he hung his head again, remembering the blood and gore that had been his life for the last year. He breathed deep, lifted his eyes to his sister, "Do you think there's any way I could talk to that Jesse fella, maybe find out about the others in the Guard?"

Rachel frowned, glanced at George and back to Reuben, "Every day, the marshal has him out sweeping the walk, picking up things, anything to get the both of them out of the office and jail for a spell. Montgomery often stops in the tavern for a drink while Jesse works." She squinted her eyes as she thought, "If you are in the store, you can watch and see when Montgomery goes for his drink, or sometimes he goes to the café to eat, then maybe you could talk to Jesse. But the marshal usually watches out the window, so, I don't know how you'll do it."

———

IT WAS MID-MORNING BEFORE THE MARSHAL ESCORTED Jesse from the jail, broom in hand, and pointed out the place of beginning two doors up from the tavern. As the young man began his daily chore, the marshal had a seat on the bench before the haberdashery. Jesse had become quite adept with the broom and the dust began to rise, giving the marshal the excuse he was waiting for as he rose and ambled to the tavern.

Reuben watched from the window of the general store across the street and as soon as the dust began to rise, he quickly made his way around the end of the street to come near the young man as he slowly worked his way down the boardwalk. He had moved from the front of the land office and now worked at the walk before the haberdashery as Reuben stepped past him and stood in the alcove of the door to the clothing store. He leaned against the side and spoke to the diligent sweeper, "Jesse, my name is Reuben."

The young man stopped sweeping and turned to frown at the stranger but Reuben motioned for him to keep sweeping. "Your friends, the Home Guard, killed my folks and burnt their farm. Nothing will happen to you, but I want their names and where they were going when they left here." He used a firm tone and a stoic expression, his head slightly bowed, giving little attention to the working man and staying clear of the door to the haberdashery.

Jesse paused and turned to scowl at Reuben, "I can't tell you that! They'll come back and do to me what they did to your folks!" he hissed.

Reuben grinned and slipped the big Bowie knife from the sheath at his back. The weapon was a wicked piece of craftsmanship, the fourteen-inch blade glistening in the morning light and the razor-sharp edge reflecting the sun. Reuben acted as if he were trimming his fingernails as he spoke softly, "I just came from the war. Killed over a hundred men, several with this Bowie knife. I got to where I could slit a man's throat just as quiet as the whisper of the morning breeze. They'd be dead before they hit the ground, never knew what happened." He paused, lifted his eyes to the young man who stood staring at this stranger with the face of death, and added, "Now, who you gonna be afraid of, your cowardly so-called friends, or this knife that has spilt more blood than all your friends combined?"

"But, but . . .," stammered Jesse, looking around, "You can't tell 'em I told you." He looked at Reuben. He frowned and asked, "You need to write it down or sumpin'?"

"Just start talkin'," scowled Reuben, eyes mere slits and a sneer splitting his face.

"Alright, there was the McNulty brothers, Frank and Jonathan. But Al, Aloysius, Thomason, he was the meanest and the leader."

"Go on," prompted Reuben.

"Then there was Wilbur Cranston, and one other, scruffy kid that just joined 'em, don't know his name. Oh, and Denton Packard, from down Indiana way."

"And where were they going?"

"Dunno for sure, but Al talked a lot about goin' to Davenport someday. Said the railroad was buildin' a bridge and lots of things were happening. Said there'd be lots of money to be made for us all." He looked toward the tavern, saw the door start to open and turned back to his broom. With his head down and his back to the street, he mumbled, "I gotta work, here comes the marshal."

Reuben stepped into the haberdashery, looked around at the clothes, casually glancing to the window for the marshal. When Montgomery returned to his seat on the bench, Reuben went to the door and stepped out, "Mornin' marshal. Nice day we're havin' isn't it?" looking up at the sky and starting across the street without waiting for an answer.

He walked into the general store and almost bumped into an anxious Rachel, who asked, "What'd he say?"

Reuben grinned, "Well, he gave me the names and where they were going."

"Where?"

"Davenport. So, I reckon I'll be getting my supplies and going to Davenport. But first, you're going to give me a description of the ragamuffins you think were the ones and we'll match names to 'em." He motioned to the back counter and they began talking like conspirators planning some special assault on the wicked of the world.

George came in from the back, saw their huddle and joined in, adding his descriptions to those of Rachel, and Reuben soon had what he needed. They stood, looking around and Reuben began listing some of the supplies he needed beginning with paper cartridges for the Sharps and his Remington Army pistol.

"Well, I don't have much. Both are in short supply, you know, war and all, and the Sharps is pretty new. But I did get some in just last week, so you're in luck." As he packed the goods into a satchel and a haversack, he looked up at Reuben, "You sure you want to sell the farm?"

"Yes, I am. Any ideas?"

George took a deep breath, glanced at Rachel, and back to Reuben. "Here's what I'll do, I will buy it from you but as soon as the banker comes, I'll sell it to him. If you could meet with him, he might give you a better price, but I don't have a lot of cash on hand. Our place was a little less than yours but I'll give you what I sold our place for and should recoup from the banker, maybe even make a bit of a profit."

"That would make it easy on me, that's for sure, and

there's nothing wrong with you making a profit, after all, it's still family." He glanced at Rachel and back at George, frowning. "When does the train come through, going west?"

George frowned, glanced at Rachel, "Today, I think." Then looking at Rachel again, "Doesn't it?"

She nodded, "But what about Rufus?"

"If they have a stock car, I'll take him with me. If not, you've got yourself a mule!" he laughed.

George frowned at Reuben, "You named the mule Rufus, like your brother?"

Both Rachel and Reuben laughed as Reuben explained, "We always said Rufus was as stubborn as a mule!"

"You're in luck! He said he can get you on the 3:10 to Chicago, then from Chicago to Davenport!" stated Rachel, excitedly. "I'm so jealous! I have wanted to take a long trip on the train ever since they came to White Pigeon!"

"What about the stock car, can I get Rufus on board?" asked Reuben, busy with packing his gear. Much of what he would carry would be bundled with his bedroll, the rest in a haversack.

"I think so but you should go talk to him; there are different tickets and such, you will have to decide about, you know, Rufus and all."

"Then I reckon I better be for gittin' down there. You walkin' with me?"

"Of course," replied Rachel, grinning at her brother as she took the crook of his arm to walk beside him.

When they arrived at the station, Reuben flipped the rein of the mule over the hitchrail and walked to the ticket window. "Howdy!" he declared as he pushed his hat back on his head. "My sister said you could get me on the next train to Chicago and on to Davenport, that right?"

The balding man looked over narrow spectacles to take in the image of the tall man before him, cocked his head to the side and said, "There's room. Whatchu want, Second Class, Third Class . . ." as he lifted his eyes up to Reuben.

Reuben let a slow grin cross his face, leaned down a mite to look directly at the seated man, "Well, first, is there a stock car that I can take my mule with me?"

"Ummhmm, cost ya though."

"And what if I want to ride with my mule?"

"Could," he started as he shuffled some rate sheets, scratched with his pencil a little then looked up at Reuben. "If you put the mule in the stock car, chances are the car will be switched at Chicago to the Chicago and Rock Island Railway to go to Davenport. You could stay aboard all the way, I reckon. But if you want, I can put you in the Second Class for a bit more, and they feedja real good."

"No, I think I like the comp'ny of my mule better'n most folks. I'll just ride with him."

"Suitchur self. That's be twelve dollars 'n fifty cents."

George had given Reuben a combination of the new Greenbacks currency and gold coin and Reuben, a little uncertain about the Greenbacks, withdrew three of the five-dollar bills and passed them through the window to the clerk. The man's eyes grew wide as he looked at the bills, then looked up at Reuben, "Heard 'bout these. First I seen of 'em. You here from the war?"

Reuben grinned, "That's right."

The man nodded and made change, all in coin, and passed it to Reuben along with the ticket. He pointed over his shoulder, "The stock car'll be loadin' at that end, so you should wait down there. Train'll be along soon 'nuff. You might wanna get some feed and water for the mule, maybe a bucket o' water. Won't be none on the train."

"Can I get that at the corrals yonder?"

"Yup, there's a man there that'll give ya a hand."

Reuben nodded again, turned away and walked with Rachel to the end of the platform. He spoke to a tender near the stock pens about some feed and water, "I can let'chu use one o' the buckets. Just leave it in the stock car when you're done."

Rachel waited while Reuben retrieved the mule and the rest of his gear. Once the mule was in the stock car, tethered and fed and watered. He stripped the gear and stacked it in a corner. There was ample hay for the mule and a stack in the corner he could use for his own bedding. He walked down the loading plank and joined Rachel on the landing platform to say his goodbyes. The steam engine was huffing and squealing as they waited for the loading of the coal and water. A sudden whistle warned of a soon departure and Rachel reached up to put her arms around her brother's neck. "Whatever you do, write me. I won't know where you are or where you're going, but I'll always be here."

Reuben bent down to wrap his arms around her waist and lift her to his level, grinning all the while. He hugged her tight and said, "You take care of that man of yours and my nephew."

"Nephew? It might be your niece!" she giggled.

Another whistle and the rattle of chains by the loading ramp prompted another quick hug, and a kiss on the whiskered cheek as Rachel said, "Don't forget we love you! You're the last of my big brothers!"

Reuben stifled a sob, choked down the difficult

goodbye and wiped the tears from his eyes as he turned away, nodding, and running for the ramp. With two long strides, he mounted the ramp and stood in the opening to watch the tenders remove the loading ramp and he waved to Rachel as the train huffed and chugged to start on its way. He leaned out to look at the retreating station, gave a last wave and sat down in the big opening of the sliding door, dangling his feet over the edge. He looked back at the mule who kept turning his head back to see where Reuben was and to maintain his footing in the clattering stock car. Reuben chuckled, "Well, Rufus, it's just me'n you boy! At least until we make a stop and maybe pick up some more stock."

The clerk had explained they would ride the Northern Indiana Railroad to Michigan City, and the car would be added to the Chicago and Rock Island train bound for Chicago. "If you're lucky, they'll just hook onto your stock car in Chicago, maybe even keep the same engine and tender, and keep you movin' until you get to Davenport. That'll be a dead-end for the Rock Island."

Reuben remembered the clerk saying they were scheduled to get to Davenport late the next day, "If things go well, it'll be around six in the evening tomorrow that you make Davenport. Now, just be prepared in case you have to off-load in Chicago and get another stock car on the Rock Island."

Reuben stood and slid the door closed part way, turned to the mule, "So, Rufus, here's hopin' we can just make this our home for the next day or so." He went to the far corner and retrieved the list he made with Rachel that gave the descriptions of the band that called themselves the Home Guard. As he read, he tried to picture each one . . .

The McNulty brothers – nothing remarkable, both dark hair, average build, but Frank has more of a mean streak, his eyes are evil!

Al (Aloysius) Thomason – the leader, always known as a bully, not known for his intelligence, but always a bit scruffy, longer hair, dirty brown, about six foot, maybe a little more, heavy build, broad shoulders. Usually wears grey linsey woolsey shirt with vest, hob-nail boots, that he uses on those he fights.

Wilbur Cranston – face like a weasel or mouse, long pointy nose, sunken cheeks, long ears, and scraggly black hair. Always wears galluses with his high-water britches, lace-up boots. Always playing with a knife.

Denton Packard – heavy brow, black hair, eyes too close together and shifty, broad flat nose, been broken too many times, tobacco-stained teeth, has a pistol in a holster but keeps a hide-a-way behind his belt at his back. He's the meanest one besides Thomason.

The light was fading and he dug out a couple of the biscuits and sausage Rachel packed for him and leaned back in the hay to consider what he was bound to do and if he would choose to go after the murderers. He pictured the farm and his family, his mother tending her rose garden, Pa coming in from the field leading the team of mules as he took off his hat and wiped his brow, Rufus coming in from milking the cow in the barn, and Rephael pushing Rachel on the swing. Then he remembered the graves, the burnt home and barn, and the promise he made to his brother, Rufus, as he breathed his last. He shook his head, knowing he had to at least try to find the band and bring them in, if possible, and if not, well, he had been well trained on how to take out an enemy. He leaned back, and with a haversack as a pillow, he let the clackety-clack of the uneven rails and the chugging and churning of the engine become his lullaby.

THE TRAIN MADE SEVERAL STOPS, EACH ONE STIRRING Reuben awake, but it was not until Michigan City when the engine and tender were replaced by ones with the markings of the Chicago and Rock Island RR and the stock car was opened and a fenced ramp put in place. A stock tender carried a section of fencing into the car and was surprised to see Reuben standing beside his mule. "Oh, didn't 'spect to see nobody in here. Wire said there was a mule but didn't say nuthin' 'bout a man."

"I paid for both the mule and me. You need to see the ticket?" answered Reuben, rubbing the sleep from his eyes.

"Nah, but you can give me a hand with this divider. We're loadin' some hogs and I reckon you don't wanna be sleepin' with them."

Reuben stepped closer to help the man but asked, "Hogs? How many?"

"Eight o' 'em. Big'uns too! You ain't gonna get no sleep with them on board."

"How far they goin'?"

"Stock yards, Chicago. You?"

"Davenport."

"Well, if they get 'em unloaded alright, they'll take this car on to Davenport, but if they don't, you'll have to change cars."

"How far to Chicago?" asked Reuben as he hooked the divider to the side wall.

"Uh, reckon it's 'bout three, four hours, dependin' on the stop at Gary."

Reuben shook his head as he watched the tender trudge down the ramp, climb the fence and motion to the others to bring the hogs. With wild squealing, grunting, and snorting, followed by the poking and yelling of the tenders, the big hogs crowded into the stock car, crashing against the divider, fighting for a place among the bedding of hay and grass. Two men leaned against the divider to crowd the hogs to the front of the stock car, latched it down and nodded to Reuben. The wide door had been slid open and one man grabbed it to close it but Reuben stopped him, "I'll close it when we get going. I think I'm gonna need all the fresh air I can stand!"

The Chicago railyards were a hubbub of activity. Even well after dark fell, engines were being serviced, oilers doing their job, engineers checking everything by the flickering light of hand-held lanterns. But the Chicago Stock Yards were not the railhead. Here the stock car was pulled alongside the stock pens and a loading chute dropped the ramp to the door of the car. Two yardhands stepped into the car, looked at the hogs and started undoing the divider, but when Reuben spoke up, one of the hands jumped and shouted. "Dad gum it! You done skeered me outta muh britches! I thought one o' them hogs was talkin'!"

Reuben chuckled at the white-eyed colored man, and stepped forward, "Can I be of help?" he asked, still chuckling.

"What'chu doin' in here?"

"Ridin' with my mule, goin' to Davenport."

The colored man shook his head, motioned to the divider, "Stand here, keep it from gettin' pushed over while we git them hogs outta here!"

The yard hand moved around the divider, grabbing

his poker stick as he crowded among the hogs, "Soooeeee pig! Soooeee!" he shouted, poking the hogs with the sharpened stick. He grabbed the tail of one, kicked it on the rump with his knee as he shouted again, "Soooeeee!" The hogs crowded one another, fighting for room to turn around and head for the big opening and when one big boar grunted, squealed, and started trotting for the chute, the others followed. Within moments the hogs were gone, the divider folded and stacked against the side wall, and the yard hands nodded and followed the hogs, leaving behind the stinking refuse.

Reuben shook his head, standing in the door and breathing deep of the air but the manure of the stock yards was not much of a change. When the engine whistled and started chugging, the jerk of the cars as the slack of the couplings was taken out, the car jerked Reuben and he had to grab onto the sliding door to keep from tumbling into the chute. But they moved just a short distance when two young colored men swung aboard, pitchforks in hand, and started cleaning out the stock car, raking the hay and manure out the door. Reuben stood by Rufus watching the young men quickly clean the car, and when they started for the hay that he used for his bed, he stopped them, "No, no. That's my bed till we get to Davenport."

"Well, suh, this train won't be pullin' outta Chicago till mornin'."

"That's alright. As long as this car is part of it!"

"Oh, it will be suh. That's why they had us cleanin' it. They's gonna have fo' of these here stock cars, the other'ns bein' empty, to go to Davenport. They be shippin' some cows back to the stock yards from there."

"Well, once I'm outta here, they can do whatever they like!" declared Reuben, nodding to the two workers as they sat down in the doorway and slid to the ground. The men had no sooner hit the ground than the engine sounded its whistle, and the line of cars shook and squealed as they headed for the railyards. Reuben assumed he wouldn't get much rest until they were bound for Davenport, and he was right. The new gas lights in the rail yard made it possible for the trains and crew to work well into the night. He watched from the doorway as the engine and tender were put on the turntable and spun around to face the opposite direction, readying it to hook onto the line of stock cars and passenger cars that would make up the train.

It was first light when the train stretched out, southward bound, to leave the railyards. Reuben counted four stock cars, two passenger cars and the caboose. He slipped his pocket watch out to look at the time and nodded as he read it to be five-thirty. "On the nose!" he mumbled, remembering the station clerk telling him they should leave Chicago at that precise time and hopefully make Davenport by 6:30 P.M.

After whistle stops at Morris, Marseilles, Ottawa, and Windsor, Reuben thought they had a straight run to Davenport, but when the whistle blew and the brakes squealed, he knew there was another stop. Genesea showed on the sign above the little station as the train came to a stop. Reuben leaned out to look at the small community, just a handful of houses, a couple businesses, two people on the landing, nothing exceptional or different from the many other whistle stops. Another whistle and the hiss of steam and scream of the drivers spinning on the rail, and the train once again stretched out, each coupling rattling and drawing tight. As Reuben turned away, a big haversack was swung up onto the floor and a big hand grabbed at the corner of the door as a booted leg in corduroy swung up, followed by a blustery man in a woolen coat and floppy hat. He rolled onto the floor of the stock car and came to hands and knees then stood to his full height which was about four inches shorter than Reuben. The men stood facing one another, both wide-eyed until the newcomer said, "Well, howdy, muh friend." He extended his hand, showed a broad smile and continued, "I am Shadrach Meshach Abednego Jones, but be careful how you says it, cuz it ain't like some folks says, it ain't Shadrach Meshach a bad negro Jones, although I have been called that oftentimes." He showed his broad grin as he doffed his hat and accepted the offered hand from a smiling Reuben.

"And I'm known as Reuben, Reuben Grundy. Welcome aboard Shadrach!"

The newcomer laughed, shook Reuben's hand and said, "It's pleased I is to meetchu Reuben."

The newcomer was shaped like a barrel although bigger than most, a streak of grey marked his hair above his left ear, smile wrinkles gathered at the corners of his eyes and mouth, dimples that looked like he'd been poked by his mother's fingers at each cheek, and another one cleft his chin. His arms filled out his woolen coat, and his legs resembled stumps, but mischief and joy radiated from his eyes.

"How far ya' goin'?" asked Reuben.

"Only till it stops!" announced Shadrach. He nodded to the corner at the front of the car and Reuben nodded his approval. The big haversack was tossed to the corner and Shad stood at the doorway, breathing deep of the afternoon air as the landscape passed by rapidly. Reuben joined him, holding to the right edge of the doorway, enjoying the scenery. The hillsides were covered in hardwood trees that were strutting the beginning of their fall colors. Orange, gold, yellow, and green blazed across the low hills and broad flats as if they were sporting a new coat of paint. Both men were seated, letting their legs dangle as Shadrach asked, "Those ain't uniform pants, is they?" frowning as he looked at the woolen britches that Reuben wore.

Reuben chuckled, "Yes, they are."

"But they's green, ain't they?"

"Ummhmm."

"Uh, the Union's blue, the south is grey, so where they from?" asked Shad, cocking one eyebrow up as he looked sidelong at his stock car mate.

Reuben chuckled, "Colonel Hiram Berdan organized the 1st Regiment of Sharpshooters. I was part of Company C, out of Michigan."

"Sharpshooters, eh? How'd you get that title?"

"Well, some volunteered, some were recruited, but all had to pass muster with ten rounds no more'n five inches from the center of the bull's eye at two hundred yards."

Shadrach whistled, shaking his head, "Now that there's some shootin', yessiree. Ten inches at two hundred yards, my oh my." He looked down at the passing fall colors, looked up at Reuben, "See any action?"

Reuben stared into the distance, remembering, took a deep breath and quietly answered, "More'n I cared too." He lifted his eyes to the distance and rattled off, "Battle of Williamsburg, Hanover Court House, and then the Seven Days of battles."

"Seven Days?"

Reuben looked at Shadrach, nodded his head, "Seven days straight, different battle each day the last seven days of June. One right after another, didn't get more'n a couple hours sleep the whole week. Lee and McClellan, Virginia," he shook his head, "seemed there were so many bodies you could walk all the way from Richmond to Malvern Hill and never touch ground."

Silence fell between the men like a heavy blanket until a big hand lightly rested on Reuben's shoulder, and the low voice of Shadrach seemed to come from the bottom of a deep well, "It's a terrible price to pay for freedom but it must be so."

Tears chased one another down Reuben's cheeks as he sat still, remembering but trying so hard to forget. He mumbled, "And they kept sending me out, working my way through the thickest woods, tasked with slowing them down, turning them back, and to do that, I had to kill men. Every time I pulled the trigger, someone died. When I took those two bullets, it was like an answer to prayer; I was relieved, but my brother died in my arms and I went home to find my family murdered and farm burned." He shook his head, "And as far as I know, there's not one man free that wasn't before all those men died. So, why?" He glanced around, stood, and returned to his bedroll in the corner for some time alone.

Shadrach stayed in the doorway, looking around, wondering, yet knowing there would be many more die before the war was over and that had prompted him to join his brother in Davenport and maybe work on the riverboats. But he had heard about something new called the Underground Railroad, and he was hopeful of becoming a conductor on that railroad. If there was to be an escape, maybe he could find it with his brother, and maybe, just maybe, he might have found a friend.

It was much more than Reuben expected to see so far west of what he knew as civilization. Davenport was a rail hub and had quickly become a center for commerce on the river as well. As the train rattled across the long bridge, he looked at the many riverboats moored at the levee, some loading lumber, others offloading other cargo. Stevedores were hoisting massive bundles onto waiting wagons, while others manhandled rough cut hardwood lumber. Beyond the levee, brick and stone buildings told of a prosperous commercial center, while smoke boiled from tall chimneys alongside industrial buildings. Reuben shook his head at the wonder of it all.

"Sumpin', ain't it? All that hurryin' 'n scurryin' about, ever'body tryin' to outdo ever'body else," rumbled the deep voice of Shadrach. The men stood side by side at the big doorway of the stockcar, watching all the activity on the levee. "Ever rode one o' those?" asked Shadrach, nodding to the riverboats.

Reuben grinned, "Nope, and can't say as I want to."

"Oh, they ain't so bad. Leastways that's what my

brother says. That's why I come here; he says he can get me on as a deck hand on one o' them boats. Says we'll go up an' down the Mississippi and get paid for it!"

"He meetin' you at the depot?"

"Nah suh, he said he'd be workin' at the livery and would wait for me there. He say we can stay there till we get on a boat."

"The livery, huh. Well, I'm gonna need a place for my mule and a place to sleep, at least for a day or two. Mind if I tag along?"

"Nah suh, that'd be just fine," replied a broad grinning Shadrach.

————

As they walked to the livery, Shadrach talked much about the settlement of Davenport. "I left here 'bout a year ago, went to Chicago to check on our mother and our only sister. 'Fore that, me and muh brother had been here, oh, 'bout six year. We helped build that Camp McClellan. It started as a recruitment center for the war, but muh brother said it's a hospital now, and they's expectin' some prisoners. That's how come they built that high fence around it.

"That big buildin' what they call the depot, that was known as the Treaty House. It's where the treaty with the Sauk or *Thakiwaki*, the Ho-Chunks or *Hocąks*, Wazijahaci, and Kickapoo was signed. But they say there's still trouble up north with some other tribes, even with the war goin' on, an' them sol'jer boys just don't know who they be gonna fight, Confederates or Indians."

They were walking on Front street, passing several businesses, and when Reuben saw one sign that said, *Police Department,* he paused, frowning, "Well, I didn't expect to see that. I thought it would be a sheriff or marshal, somethin' like that."

"You got bizness wit' the police?" asked a frowning Shadrach.

"Prob'ly not, more like the sheriff of the county, I reckon," answered Reuben, continuing their stroll in the dusk of the day. The western sky was showing dim colors of the sunset as they rounded the corner to see the big livery barn. It stood taller than any of the nearby structures, the double doors at the front standing wide open and the rear doors showing enough light to see the corrals behind the barn.

Standing at the big door was the spitting image of Shadrach, one hand on his hip, the other on the door, a big grin splitting his face and showing white teeth. The two men stepped close, both laughing as they bumped bellies and hugged one another. Shadrach turned to Reuben, "This here's muh brother, Mordecai Methuselah Jones!" he nodded to Reuben, turned to his brother, "And this is my new friend, Reuben Grundy!"

Reuben stepped forward, grinning, and accepted the meaty paw of the big man, "Pleased to meet you, Mordecai."

"And you too, Reuben." He craned around to look at the mule, "That's a fine lookin' mule you got there, wanna sell him?"

"I can't sell him, that's Rufus, named him after my dear departed brother of the same name."

All three men chuckled and Shadrach interjected, "I tol' him we'd have a stall for him and Rufus, if'n that's alright."

"Course it is, brother, course it is." He turned back to Reuben, "You just take your brother right on back to the first empty stall and make yourself ta' home!"

THE SIGN HANGING OVER THE WINDOWS READ *MAMA Riley's boarding and eating house.* With a broad smile and high expectations, Reuben stepped through the door and was instantly greeted by a smiling, rosy-cheeked, buxom woman with a touch of grey in her hair and an apron over her ample front. "Evenin' friend, step in and have a seat!" She motioned toward an empty table among the many occupied tables and Reuben nodded and walked to the offered chair and table. The woman followed and when he was seated, she added, "I'm Mama Riley, and our special tonight is roast pork, potatoes and gravy, fresh green beans, baked butternut squash, and our fluffy sourdough rolls."

"That sounds wonderful!" nodded Reuben as he scooted his chair up to the table.

"I'll bring it right out. Oh, and if we get crowded, would you mind sharing your table?"

"At your pleasure, ma'am," answered Reuben, smiling, and nodding.

It was but a moment before she returned, smiling broadly, and carrying an overloaded plate and a smaller plate with two large rolls. She sat them down and the aroma of fine food filled the air around Reuben, much to his delight. She quickly returned with a big cup and a pot of coffee, poured the cup full, and stood back, "So, young man, you think that'll do ya?"

"Yes ma'am. I haven't had a meal like this since I sat down at my mother's table!"

"And how long has that been?"

"Well, 'fore I left for the war, so that'd be late June, last year," answered Reuben, reaching for the coffee.

"And why, pray tell, are you not at her table now?"

Reuben dropped his head and softly answered, "She's in Heaven now, with my father and two brothers."

A sorrowful frown immediately painted the woman's face as she seemed to melt where she stood. She sat the pot down, and seated herself at the table beside Reuben, reached out and touched his hand, "Oh, I'm so sorry."

Reuben nodded, choking on his thoughts, and reached for the linen napkin and tucked it in the neck of his shirt, reaching for the utensils. He smiled at Mama Riley, "Thank you, ma'am."

She frowned, looking sorrowfully at the young man before her and added, "And I see not only sadness but resolve in your eyes. What is it you're about, lad?"

He sighed heavily, cutting the meat into bite-sized chunks, looked at her and said, "Those that done it are on the run and I'm honor bound to find them."

"So it wasn't the war?"

"No, ma'am. My older brother and I were gone to the war, he was killed and I was wounded, but when I returned, the family farm was burned and the rest of my family were dead."

"Well, who dunnit, then?"

"A pack o' layabouts and ne'er do wells that pretended to be the Home Guard and set about taking what they wanted from the others that stayed behind."

She shook her head, gritting her teeth to keep from saying what she felt, then looked up at Reuben. "Is that what your dear mother would be wantin' you to do?"

"Well, I know this. I know my father and brothers would be wantin' me to do it. But my mother would probably be quotin' some scripture about forgiveness but I just can't seem to find it in me. Even though I'm almighty tired of killin', I feel I've got to stop them from doin' anymore of what they done."

"Well, the stoppin' of it I can understand. Wouldn't want no one else to have to suffer that. Is that what brought you here? You on their trail?"

"All I know is they had talked about coming to Davenport. When they left White Pigeon, no one rightly knew where they went but one of their former number said they talked about Davenport. So, here I am."

Mama Riley nodded her head, looked around, and stood with coffeepot in hand, "Now, don't you leave 'fore I finish talkin' to you. There's somethin' you need to know."

When she returned, she sat down and leaned toward Reuben, "Sheriff Thorington is a good friend of mine. Now, what you must do is first thing tomorrow . . ." and she lined out what she thought would be Reuben's best chance at getting all the information the sheriff had and possibly get his help in the hunt for the outlaws. When she finished, she added, "Now, you be sure to tell him I sent you and you'll get all the help he can give. He's a good man." She nodded to Reuben, stood, and smiled at him, patted his shoulder, and returned to the kitchen.

"Yes suh, it's right on Bolivar Square, when you gets there, you can't miss it!" declared Mordecai. "You just take your time, ol' Rufus'll be just fine right'chere."

Reuben chuckled, "Well, dependin' on what the Sheriff has to say, I might leave as early as this afternoon."

"That's fine, no hurry!" answered Mordecai.

Reuben started his trek of about eight blocks with the morning sun off his left shoulder as it peeked through the business buildings and fine homes. As he neared Bolivar Square, the homes gave way to brick business buildings, picket fences yielded to broad board walks, but the stench of refuse in the muddy streets had convinced Reuben to find his way out of town as soon as possible. He climbed the steps to the stately courthouse. He recognized the Greek Revival style of the two-story brick structure and admired the columns and round cupola. It was an impressive building and to Reuben, unexpected this far west.

As he stepped through the doors, he spotted a directory and soon found the Scott County Sheriff's Office.

When he pushed through the door that stood ajar, he was greeted by a smartly dressed woman in a long skirt, ruffled long-sleeved blouse, and a broad smile beneath bright eyes. "May I help you, sir?"

Reuben quickly doffed his hat and nodded, "Yes ma'am," but was stopped by the brunette with hair piled high, "It's miss, Miss Stapleton," she stated firmly, pointing at the name plate that rested near the edge of the first desk.

"Uh, pardon me," stammered Reuben, "I'd like to see the sheriff, if I may?"

"And who shall I say is calling?"

Reuben frowned, asked, "Calling?"

"Your name, sir."

"Oh, Reuben Grundy. And tell him that Mama Riley told me to come see him."

"And may I ask what this is about?"

"About a gang of murderers calling themselves the Home Guard."

Her eyes flared and she cocked her head to the side, motioned for him to be seated, and briskly turned away to stride to the closed door that had the name, *James Thorington, Sheriff*, painted on the frosted glass. She rapped two times and opened the door and stepped through, closing the door behind her. Momentarily, she returned, motioned to Reuben, "The sheriff will see you now."

Reuben rose and pushed his way past the swinging divider and walked to the open door, stepped into the office, and heard the door close behind him. Behind the desk, the seated man bore a dark brown goatee and mustache, thick hair parted on the side that covered the tops of his ears and piercing brown eyes. He cocked one eyebrow up as he gave Reuben a once over, motioned him to the chair and as Reuben was seated, "What's this about a Home Guard?"

Reuben leaned slightly forward and explained what he found when he returned home in White Pigeon and what he discovered from the one man left behind. "When they did their deeds in White Pigeon, there were five of them." He handed the sheriff a copy of his list of names and descriptions.

"And you're on their trail?"

Reuben dropped his eyes, sighed heavily, and looked up at the sheriff, "I promised my brother on his death bed I would take care of Ma and Pa. But when I got home, they were dead. Now I feel honor-bound to at least find those that killed them and burnt the farm, do what I can to bring them to justice. The word was they were coming to Davenport, so . . ."

"What'd you do in the war, since you're already out?"

"I was in Company C, 1st Regiment, of Berdan's Sharpshooters. I'm only out because I took two bullets at the battle of Malvern Hill."

"I heard about the Sharpshooters. Good outfit." He stared at Reuben, thinking, then asked, "I see by that bulge in your coat you're carryin' a sidearm, anything else?"

"I have a Bowie Knife but my rifle is with my gear at the livery."

"Rifle?"

"A '59 Sharps, paid for it myself so I was able to keep it when I mustered out."

"The sidearm?"

Reuben pulled away his jacket to reveal the holstered pistol, "Remington Army revolver, .44."

"Would the sheriff at White Pigeon vouch for you?"

"Not sure, most think he was partners with the gang

of thieves that called themselves the Home Guard. He didn't do anything about all they did, didn't go after them, didn't even question the one left behind who was in his jail."

"Hmmm," grumbled the Sheriff, nodding and looking at a telegram that lay on his desk.

"Well, Reuben Grundy, let me tell you what I know." He paused, looked up at Reuben, and continued, "I think your boys came through town here, couple weeks ago there was a disturbance at the edge of town, an isolated home. But what the bunch hadn't counted on, our folks have taken to entertaining some of the recruits at Camp McClellan and there were half-dozen of 'em just sittin' down to dinner when those boys rode up and demanded 'taxes to support the war'. The man of the house said they were already supportin' the war since their two sons had enlisted. But they got a little belligerent and demanded money. That's when the six soldier boys lined out on the porch and sort of dared them fellas to try to collect but they saw the error of their ways and left."

"Two weeks?" asked Reuben.

But the sheriff held up his hand to stop his questions, and continued, "Didn't think much of it until I got this telegram a few days back. It's from a deputy up in Durant, that's about three hours ride, it says *Band of outlaws calling themselves Home Guard and demanding taxes for the war. Burning homes and killing people that refuse. Two homes burnt, two dead. Same in Fulton.* The sheriff lifted his eyes to Reuben, "Sounds like your boys, don't it?"

Reuben nodded.

"Problem is Fulton and Durant are in Muscatine and Cedar counties. And the last thing we want if for Iowa to become a haven for Jayhawkers and Red Legs! We can't have this kind of stuff getting out of hand! And the war has taken most of the fightin' men and left us with old men and others to serve as deputies. All the regiments formed at Camp McClellan are bound for the fight in the south and east and we don't need to have 'em chasin' down a bunch of Bushwhackers! And after that John Brown did what he did, there's no tellin' what the sympathies of some folks are now. So, now, all the counties honor neighboring counties and their lawmen but I can't leave here and go chasing after a bunch that's probably headin' west faster'n I could. And if I were to catch 'em, I'd be so far away from my county, no tellin' what might happen here with me gone."

Reuben replied, "I understand sir. Well, the information about where they are is a help."

"Now hold your horses, I'm not finished." The sheriff leaned forward on his desk and said, "Here's what I can do." He reached to the side into an open drawer and brought out something he held obscured in his hand. He grinned at Reuben, "I can make you a deputy and your authority will be recognized in all the counties in most of Iowa. This is not a license," he held up the badge for Reuben to see, "but it might help you when you catch up to 'em, as long as they're still in Iowa, but the rest will be up to you. If you can bring 'em into any of the sheriff's offices, they can take it from there. I'll have some warrants made out if you'll leave me their names and descriptions. But, and this is important, I want you to keep me apprised of your progress real regular like, understand?"

Reuben was sitting straight, trying to absorb what the Sheriff was saying and nodded a simple "uh huh," and looked at the sheriff, disbelief showing on his face.

"Now, by regular, I mean ever couple days or so I want a telegram from you. Got it?"

"Uh, yes sir, I reckon so, sir," answered Reuben, nodding but still sitting straight and unmoving.

The sheriff chuckled and said, "Now stand up and hold up your hand so we can get you sworn in."

Reuben did as instructed, repeated the vow of office after the sheriff and accepted the badge, still disbelieving.

The sheriff chuckled again, "Now, this pays thirty dollars a month, plus expenses and ammunition. So, if you'll go down to Wheeler's Emporium, they can fix you up with anything you need. I'll have the warrants waiting for you at Wheeler's." He handed the telegram to Reuben, "That'll help you identify yourself when you stop in the sheriff's office in Durant, if you do. Now, good luck and good hunting!"

Reuben turned around and walked out of the office, still in a daze and disbelieving what just happened. He heard a giggle from beside him and glanced at the office girl as she put her hand to her mouth, watching him leave the office. Reuben shook his head, replaced his hat, and exited the courthouse to face the bright sun direct in his face. He shook his head again and started for the livery.

"Guess I'll need to get Rufus, maybe a packhorse, and get more supplies. Reckon I'll be travelin' a while," he mumbled to himself, oblivious to the people walking past and staring at him. When he walked into the livery, he was pinning the deputy's badge on his shirt and the two brothers stared. "What'chu gone and done?" asked Shadrach.

"I'm not sure, Shad. I just walked into his office to see if he knew anything about that bunch I'm after, and next thing I know I was walkin' out with this badge in hand. Darnedest thing ever happened to me!"

"We've thought 'bout joinin' up, but, well, we might be gettin' a little too old. After all, Mordecai there is almost as old as his namesake, Methuselah, and I ain't too far behind," drawled Shadrach, looking at Reuben.

Reuben stopped rigging the new mule's packsaddle and turned to look at the brothers, he grinned, shook his head, "I heard they were gettin' up a colored regiment but I think you might be right. I s'pose that white hair might show your age." He chuckled as he turned back to his task.

Shadrach touched his white streak, laughed a deep belly laugh, "Why, that ain't age, that's wisdom bustin' out!"

"Well, between the two of you, that's enough wisdom to keep you outta the war! 'Sides, you might have some folks drop by lookin' for freedom that you might oughta help, if you know what I mean."

The two brothers grinned, nodded, glanced at each other, and Shadrach answered, "Yes suh, we know what'chu mean."

Reuben finished rigging the packsaddle and the mule he purchased from Mordecai, turned back to his friends, extending his hand to shake, "It's been a pleasure getting to know you fellas. We prob'ly won't see each other again, so, take care of each other, ya'hear?"

Shadrach dropped his eyes, slowly lifting his head to look at Reuben with a somber expression, "I have a question for you, young man. If you was to go out there after them Bushwhackers and get yourself kilt, do you know you'd go to Heabin'?

Reuben frowned, shook his head, "Ya know, there was a time that I would have answered that question right off and tell you yes I do, but . . ." he paused, shaking his head, "after what I've done in the war and what I've felt," he shook his head again, "and what I've said to God, I just don't know if He'd have me."

The men fell silent, waiting for Reuben to say more but when nothing came, Shadrach spoke quietly, "Just remember, son, God don't never leave you. If you ever asked Him into your heart to be your Savior, He won't never leave! So, anytime you think God seems far away, guess who moved!"

Reuben breathed deep, looked up at the brothers and let a slow smile split his face. He stuffed his foot in the stirrup of the McClellan saddle and swung aboard Rufus, looked down at the two, "Be seein' you fellas!" tipped his hat and slapped legs to the big mule and left the barn with only one glance over his shoulder at the brothers.

He reined up in front of Wheeler's Emporium, tied off the mules and walked into the big store. He was instantly assaulted by smells of leather, powder, sweaty bodies, and the many other odors of leather gear, traps, rigs, and more. He saw two men behind a long counter that sat in front of a back wall of rifles and shotguns and walked to the counter. One of the men, a tall lean man with a hatchet face and eyes too close together that barely showed under thick eyebrows, scowled at Reuben, giving him a once over before asking, "And what do you need?"

"Sheriff Thorington sent me to you to get all the supplies I need for a little jaunt I'm undertaking," began Reuben as he looked the lanky clerk up and down. The man's expression changed at the name of the sheriff and he leaned forward against the counter and nodded at Reuben to give his list.

He began, "First, I need some paper cartridges for my Sharps .52, and my Remington .44. Then I'll take some . . ." and he continued to name off his list of needed supplies. Both clerks hopped to and began stacking the gear and supplies on the counter, then the smaller of the two started writing down and tallying up the amount. When they finished, he looked at Reuben, "You payin' or is the Sheriff?"

"He said to show you this," he peeled back his jacket to show the deputy badge, "and you'd just send him the bill."

Both clerks nodded and grinned, the lanky one leaning over to check the list and tally, nodding and pushed the list before Reuben, "Sign it or make your mark!"

Reuben slowly shook his head, leaned down to examine the list and looked at the little one, "Uh, you either forgot the second box of Sharp's cartridges, or you put too many down." The man stuttered, frowned, and looked at the list, then with a quick glance to the lanky man, he dispatched him to the back room for more cartridges. When the second box hit the counter, Reuben nodded, signed the list, and said, "Thank you gentlemen."

With his arms full, he took the first load out to the pack mule, returned for the second load and the lanky man offered his help. When they stepped beside the mule, the panniers were full, but Reuben had procured a sizeable haversack to tie down atop the packsaddle and the rest of the supplies filled up the bag and was quickly secured.

The clerk stood on the boardwalk while Reuben checked the load, ensuring everything was secure and stepped beside Rufus. As he started to mount, the clerk cleared his voice and spoke quietly, "Thanks for not making an issue of that extra box, he tries that too often and he's bound to get in trouble but I can't say anything. You know how it is, he could fire me and money's scarce."

"So's character," replied Reuben as he stepped aboard his mule. He pulled Rufus' head around and headed out of town. He shook his head as he left, anxious to put the city behind him. He carried a crude map, given him by the sheriff, and he took to a well-traveled road that pointed northwest. The roadway paralleled the railway, often obscured by the thick timber and other greenery. He noticed elm, oak, and occasional hackberry, some willow and birch. With undergrowth thick with chokecherry, elderberry and willows, the woods round about were thick and oftentimes appeared impenetrable. One hilly area showed oak, maple and sycamore, tall trees that stood firm against any breeze that ruffled the leaves. Beyond the thicker trees, an occasional break in the woods showed cleared and planted fields, farmhouses and barns of places that were well established and proven up.

He was less than two hours out of Davenport when he spotted the corner of a cleared field surrounded by fencing of stacked rocks and poles, common in land cleared by hand. But the fields appeared untended, and his curiosity aroused, he reined up, and with the mules tethered away from the roadway, he pushed through the brush and woods to stand at the edge of the fence. He shook his head as he saw the burnt remains of a once prosperous farm. But the destruction appeared recent, nothing was overgrown, and the bloated carcass of a cow lay in the yard between the remains of the barn and the house. He turned back to the mules, mounted up and rode further on the roadway, watching for a road that would take him back to the farm.

Within moments, he was reliving the carnage at his own family's place as he stood at the edge of the family plot that held three fresh graves and crude markers. The names showed a husband and wife and a young girl, the Mullican family. The dates showed just the years of birth and death, but the soil atop the mounds was still dark with moisture, showing they could not be more than two, three days old. He did a quick walk around, looking for anything that would help him in his search, but the tracks of many horses and a few buggies and wagons had covered any from the perpetrators. He looked around, trying to spot any neighboring properties, and he thought he saw a thin spiral of smoke, maybe from a cookstove, and he mounted up to find the neighbor.

———

"I'M TELLIN' YOU, FRANK, THERE WEREN'T NO CAUSE TO kill that girl!"

Frank McNulty scowled at his brother Jonathan, curled his lip, "Quit'cher whinin', Jon, we couldn't leave her to tell about us! She could hang us all!"

"What're you two grousin' about?" asked Al Thomason, the leader of the little band of raiders. Thomason had become the leader of the band of raiders because of his experience with Jennison's Jayhawkers in the free state of Kansas. He had been one of the early followers of Charles Jennison when he was known as a Jayhawker and looted and sacked the farms and villages on the border of Missouri. But when Jennison chose to become 'respectable' and form a regiment of volunteers for the war, Thomason took his leave and fled to Iowa, following the trail of the early abolitionist John Brown. But Brown had been hung by the time Thomason came to Iowa and he continued to Chicago and Michigan where he organized his band of followers to pick up the ways of the Jayhawkers, under the guise of being Free-Staters.

"Ain't nuthin'!" declared Frank, "Jon's just askin' 'bout that girl you kilt the other day an' I explained 'bout witnesses an' such."

"You got any complaints, you bring 'em to me, unner-stan'?" shouted Thomason. "I tol' you we'd make out real good and we have, an' it's only gonna get better! Ain'tchu noticed, ain't nobody on our trail. We can do what we want, cuz all the men have joined up and become sol'-jers!" He accented his remark with a belly laugh, slapping his leg as they rode toward their next prey. They had settled into a routine; scout out the farm, hit it just before dark, take everything and burn what's left. No one lives to tell.

"With no one after us, why can't we hit more places, get more stuff an' money?" whined Wilbur Cranston, the mousy one of the bunch.

"That's why there ain't nobody after us. We hit too many too close and all the neighbors will get together and come after us. We don't need that kinda fight, cuz ain't nobody fights as hard as a bunch o' neighbors out for vengeance. This way, by the time of our next hit, won't be the same neighbors to come huntin' us!" explained Thomason.

Wilbur cackled, looked at the rider beside him, "Hey, Denton, ain't he the smart one?"

Denton Packard had no concerns about somebody coming after them and no respect for the leader of their group. He rode along for whatever he could get for his share and he usually took a little more and, if he had to, he would kill any of these he rode with just to take a bigger share. He shook his head and mumbled, "Don't mean nuthin' to me!"

"What'd you say?" whined Wilbur, leaning closer.

"Oh shut up, Mouse!" growled Denton, shaking his head at the weasel-looking man. He had been tasked with leading the only packhorse, loaded with some of their plunder. They usually only took money and weapons but, occasionally, something that appeared especially valuable would catch the eye of their leader and he would stuff whatever it was in one of the panniers on the packhorse. They carried few supplies, taking what they needed from the farms they hit, often eating the meals that had been prepared for their victims and they ate while the bodies of their prey lay nearby.

Jonathan and Frank McNulty rode behind Al Thomason, their leader, and Jonathan leaned over and whispered to his brother, "How many more farms you think we'll hit 'fore we hightail it outta the country?"

"How would I know? What difference does it make, the more we hit, the more we get!"

"Yeah, reckon you're right. But I don't fancy gettin' caught neither," groused his brother.

"We ain't gonna get caught! Al's purty smart and we done alright so far, ain't we?"

"Yeah, I reckon, but I was thinkin', you know that ever'body ever got caught didn't think they'd get caught neither, but they did, didn't they?"

"Look, Jon, long as we play it smart, we ain't gonna get caught and we can keep this up as long as the war is on. Folks'll think we're part of their Home Guard, just like Al says. We'll hit 'nuff places to get us a good bunch o' money, and maybe we can go out west somewhere, maybe Oregon or Californy."

Jon nodded, grinning, "I heard they struck gold in Californy. Maybe we could get us some gold, ya' think?"

Frank nodded, "Sure Jon, we can get us some gold from them miners just like we get the money from these farmers, take it!" he cackled at the thought and Jon's expression.

Jon shook his head, dropped his eyes, and thought about what they were doing. He didn't like the killing. He understood why they did it but that didn't make it any easier. He hadn't personally killed anyone and didn't want to, but he also knew Al and his brother were watching him and would probably expect him to be just as involved as they were and he wasn't sure he could do that.

He didn't mind the stealing, for he always thought if someone couldn't fight to keep their goods, they didn't deserve to keep it, and he would gladly take it from them. But killing just wasn't right, taking somebody's money was one thing but taking their life was different. He thought of his mother who had tried to teach the boys to do right but their father had taught them the ways of thievery. Both were dead now, their father hung for killing a neighbor and their mother from working herself to death to support the boys. While he missed his mother, his brother, Frank, resented her for being weak and dying. Jon shook his head at the remembrance, glanced at his brother, and lapsed into one of his surly and quiet moods.

As Reuben rode up the long roadway that led to the neighbor's farm, he was greeted by two barrels protruding from the curtained windows on either side of the doorway. He reined up and leaned forward on the rounded pommel of the saddle, pushed his hat back and called out, "Hello the farm! I'm friendly, just lookin' to water my animals and maybe get some information!"

"Who are you and where you from?" called a man's voice from within the farmhouse.

"I'm Deputy Grundy, from Scott County Sheriff's office. I'm on the trail of some raiders that have been hittin' farms, burnin' 'em out and killin' some. I'd like to ask you some questions, if I might?"

"Go 'head on an' water your mules. I'm comin' out!" called the man, then spoke quietly to his woman, "Keep your gun on him, Ma. Just in case."

Reuben chuckled when he heard the man's warning to his woman but he stepped down and led the mules to the water trough that sat before the pump. It had ample water and Reuben saw no reason to use the pump, so he stood beside Rufus and watched the man come from the farm house. He appeared to be middle-aged, bald with just the fringe of hair above his ears, his head and neck well-tanned from the work in the field. His high-water britches showed rough lace boots; pillow ticking had been used to make his britches and his cotton shirt showed sweat and dirt from his labor in the field. He shaded his eyes, looking at Reuben, "Deputy, huh? I'm Josiah Jamison, this is my place. My woman, Lydia, is inside with a rifle on you."

Reuben pulled back his jacket to show the badge, "That's right. And I did notice your wife's rifle sticking out the window," he replied, grinning. "What can you tell me about what happened to your neighbor?" nodding toward the burnt-out farm.

"The Mullicans. The ol' man, Hector, his wife, Mildred, and their grandchild, Suzie. Their son, Hector Jr., joined up and left her with 'em, her ma died givin' birth." He paused, looked up at Reuben and continued, "Don't know much, didn't see nobody, and by the time we saw the fire and went to runnin', whoever done it was gone. We did hear some runnin' horses on the road but, as you know, this roadway's a mite fer from the main road where they was, so, we didn't see 'em. We, and some other neighbors buried 'em the next day. That was three days back."

"Did you see any sign of what the raiders did, how many there were, anything?"

"What they did was kill 'em and burnt the house down 'round 'em. We played hob getting' the bodies outta there to bury 'em. Had to, they was stinkin' awful." He shook his head as he remembered, "They kilt the live-stock, 'ceptin' the horse, took him I reckon, but kilt the milk cow and pigs. Chickens just ran off, prob'ly turn up 'round here soon 'nuff."

"Do you know of any other places the raiders might have hit?"

"Dunno, nobody close by, but beyond hereabouts, no tellin'. Ain't been into town in a couple weeks. Might hear sumpin' then."

"Well, sorry to bother you. I best be movin' on; it'll take some doin' to catch up with 'em."

Jamison nodded, stepped back, and cradled his rifle in the crook of his arm. As Reuben mounted up and tipped his hat to the man and nodded to the window, the farmer turned away to return to his home. Reuben started down the roadway, wondering about the futility of his chase. Walcott was nothing more than a whistle stop with a water tower and shack with a stack of wood behind. Fulton was little more with one general store and a blacksmith. Reuben stopped at the blacksmith, watered the mules and spoke with the smithy, "I'm on the trail of a band of raiders callin' themselves the Home Guard and robbin' and killin' folks and burnin' farms. Last I heard, there were five of 'em. They hit a farm on the other side of Walcott 'bout three days ago. You see anybody like that come through here?"

The big man, a leather apron over his ample middle, bare shoulders and arms that were thick with black hair, and a drooping mustache that marred his face, glowered at Reuben, "Who're you?"

"I'm Deputy Grundy, outta Scott County."

"Yeah, I seen 'em. Rough lookin' bunch but they didn't bother me," he flexed his chest and biceps to explain why they left him alone and Reuben clearly understood. He thought anything less than an on-the-prod bull bison would readily choose to leave this man alone. "They rode through here, five of 'em with one packhorse, loaded. They was in a hurry, kicked up a lotta dust and rode out like the devil hisself was after 'em." He frowned, glaring at Reuben, "That be you?" he asked.

"If I catch 'em, they'll think that."

"That was, lessee, this is Thursday, so that was Tuesday mornin' early. I was just gettin' the fire goin'. Looked to be headin' to Durant. There's a deputy there might be able to help."

Reuben nodded, mounted up and looked at the man who now stood close to eye to eye with him but Reuben noticed he was standing on a broad flat stump to give him better access to the fire. "Thanks for the information and the water for the mules." He reined the mule away from the trough as the smithy replied, "Hope you get 'em!" Reuben nodded again nudging the mule to the roadway.

Dusk was lowering its curtain as Reuben rode into Durant. It was not much more than the last town but in addition to the general store, there was a sheriff's office, a post office, a livery, and a tavern and a few homes behind. He stopped in front of the sheriff's office, saw the open door, and stepped down as he wrapped the reins of the mules around the hitchrail. He stepped up on the boardwalk and walked into the office to see a man hunched over the desk, a cold cup of coffee before him, as he shuffled through some papers. The man looked up, surprised, grinned, "Howdy! What'chu need?"

"You the sheriff?"

"Nah, I'm just the deputy. Parker's the name," he explained as he stood and extended his hand. Reuben shook the man's hand as he introduced himself, "I'm Reuben Grundy. Sheriff Thorington down to Scott County received this," handing the telegram to the deputy.

Parker looked at the telegram, nodded, and looked up at Reuben, "You a deputy?"

"Ummhmm. What can you tell me 'bout those places?"

Parker motioned for him to be seated and sat down himself, put his elbows on the desk and leaned forward, "Well, not much more'n I said in the telegram. There were two places I know of that got hit, weren't nobody home at the one but, the other'n, they killed a widow woman and her son. Near as we could tell, they took ever'thing of value 'fore they torched the place, even kilt the livestock. Weren't no need of that, but they done it."

"Anybody see 'em?"

"One o' the neighbors said he saw several men ridin' down the road at a purty good clip but that was 'fore he knowed what happened. Said he thought there was five of 'em, one packhorse. He was comin' in from the field an' they didn't see him. Prob'ly a good thing."

"What direction were they going?" asked Reuben.

"West, maybe Moscow, Peedee, or West Liberty. Beyond that if they follow the railway, they'll come to Iowa City."

"The farms they hit, were they just off the road, but close enough to be seen?"

"Mmmhmm," he answered, nodding, and frowning.

"Any deputies in the towns you mentioned?"

"Were before the war but ain't nobody left to do the job. Next office of the law is in Iowa City." He frowned, looking at Reuben, then asked, "You goin' after 'em?"

"Yup. But it's too late to go further today. That livery, big enough to take in my mules and me?"

"It is. But if you want, you can take one o' these cots here, if you don't mind sleepin' in the jail," suggested Parker, grinning.

"That's all right. My mules would miss me if I got too far away from 'em and I'll be startin' out purty early. Any place to eat around here?"

"The tavern yonder puts out some good food, best in town. Course, it's the only food in town," chuckled the deputy. "Go 'head on and put up your mules. I'll close up and meet'chu over there, how'll that be?"

"That'll be fine and I need to send a telegram to the sheriff," answered Reuben, rising to send the report to Sheriff Thorington and go to the mules and the livery.

The rising sun warmed his back as it peeked through the heavy foliage on the over-arching trees above the roadway. It promised to be a good day, the mules were frisky and stepped out at a brisk pace, and Reuben felt good after a warm night's sleep and a good breakfast at the tavern. He kept a wary eye out, looking for evidence of the passing of the raiders but had also been warned the farther west he went the greater the possibility of running into some of the Sauk or the Ho-Chunk Indians. He was told by Sheriff Thorington the Ho-Chunks were friendly, but there were always a few that did their best to make life miserable for the white man they saw as invaders to their land. He also heard the Santee Sioux further north were raiding the white settlements, stealing food and animals for their people since the government was not living up to their part of the treaty.

He was startled when a bobcat chased a rabbit across the road in front of them but the big mule just twitched his ears and did not miss a step. Reuben chuckled and admonished himself to keep his attention on the here and now and not be thinking about rare possibilities of meeting up with any Indians. It was just past mid-morning when Reuben rode into the bustling little town of Moscow. The main street was crowded with farm wagons and horses; there were several businesses, a mercantile, two taverns, a sheriff's office that shared a building with a dentist/barber, and the ever-present livery/blacksmith. Several clapboard houses were crowded together trying to share the shade of the few trees that remained after the railway built their bridge and the boom that accompanied the coming of the railway. But regardless of the sudden growth, it was already showing signs of demise with two buildings boarded up and one partially burned. The burned remnants showed a charred sign that told it was once a hotel.

Reuben reined up in front of the sheriff's office and saw a badge-wearing man hustling out of the doorway, looking a little frantic as he talked with a man beside him. Reuben spoke up, "Are you the sheriff?"

The man frowned, "Whaddayou want?"

"Well, if you're the sheriff," started Reuben, pulling back the flap of his jacket to show his badge, "I'd like to talk to you a moment. It's important."

"Then follow me to the livery to get my horse; I got to get outta town to see a farm yonder. There's been a killin'!" he growled as he stomped down the boardwalk.

"Might be the same bunch I'm after!" declared Reuben, keeping pace with the harried sheriff.

Reuben's statement stopped the man dead in his tracks and he spun around and said, "Same bunch you're after?"

"I'm on the trail of a band of raiders callin' themselves the Home Guard that are attacking isolated farms, killin' ever'body, stealin' what they can, and burnin' everything to the ground."

"How many?" growled the man, his drooping mustache dancing at the corners of his mouth as he spoke.

"Five, maybe more."

"Come on then!" he motioned as he turned and stretched out toward the livery.

As the sheriff moved away, Reuben called after him, "I'll get my mules and be right along!" and turned to trot back to the mules. He quickly swung aboard and pulled Rufus' head around and dug heels to his ribs to get to the livery before the sheriff was gone. As he approached the big doors of the livery at the end of the street, the sheriff came out at a trot, saw Reuben, and waved him to come alongside.

"We'll take the railroad bridge, it's quicker," then he looked at the mules and back at Reuben, "if you're mules will take it, that is. It's safe enough, but it's noisy on them planks. My horse is used to it and it don't bother him but some animals spook at it."

"If you're horse takes to it, the mules will follow easy enough," declared Reuben, more hopeful than certain. When they neared the bridge, both mules twitched their long ears, lifted their heads, and gave the river and the bridge the once over, but when the sheriff rode his mount straight on between the tracks, the mules followed. It was a common practice and a goodwill gesture to the communities that the railroads often made the bridges with solid planking to enable horses and even buggies and wagons to use the bridges but posted signs as to the right-of-way of the trains. The mules were a little skittish, often giving the noisy planks a cautious look, but they were not to be outdone by the sheriff's horse and valiantly followed on across the bridge.

Once across, the sheriff motioned Reuben to come alongside and as he did, he asked, "Tell me what you know of this bunch, if it is the same bunch."

"Well, the first I knew of them was after they hit my folks place and a few others in Michigan!" He continued telling the sheriff what he knew of the five men and about the farms they plundered this side of Davenport. "It appears they hit one, move on a day or two, hit another, and keep going. I think their plan is to stretch out the damage, so no community gets too upset and puts together a posse or something. I also think they are well aware that most places have all too few fighting men and most sheriff's offices are undermanned."

"And how many places you passed comin' here?"

"Four."

"And you're the only one goin' after 'em?"

"Appears so, but Sheriff Thorington made out some warrants for 'em."

"All because most our offices have only one sheriff or deputy on account of the war," grumbled the angry sheriff.

"What were you told about the place where we're headed?" asked Reuben.

"Bout the same thing. A farm was hit, folks killed, place burned."

They smelled the stench of burnt flesh before they saw the smoldering rubble. Both men slipped their neckerchiefs up over their noses as they rode closer to the burnt home, barn, and other sheds. Everything had fallen in, smoke still twisted up and away, buzzards were circling but would not come near with the smoke and now with people and animals moving about. The men tied off their mounts at the edge of the trees and, slowly shaking their heads, started to the pile of black that once was a home. Singed rose bushes, leaves burnt, held to one blackened bloom, reminding Reuben of his mother's garden. As they drew near, Reuben let the sheriff take the lead and start picking through the debris. Within moments, they found the remains of a man and a woman, bodies charred and bloated. The sheriff started coughing and spitting, moved away quickly and emptied his guts on the ground beside the burnt timbers. He shook his head, wiped his face, and stood, looking at the sky, and sucking air trying for a breath of freshness but failing. Reuben turned away, hardened to the sight from the war and the more recent discoveries of the other farms. He walked to the packhorse and stripped off the shovel, strode along the tree line for any evidence of a family grave plot but finding none, picked a spot and started digging.

———

"Looks likely," said Frank McNulty, standing beside Thomason as they peered through the trees at the farmhouse. It sat back away from the road, backed up to the river, thick trees roundabout and brushy hedgerows dividing the fields.

"That ol' man's doin' all the work, so prob'ly ain't no other men about. That ol' lady at the clothesline won't be no trouble," observed Thomason. He glanced at the lowering sun, "It's about dusk now, we could go 'head on an' hit 'em, be long gone by dark."

"Place looks to be in good shape, old folks prob'ly got a good stash of money some'eres," suggested McNulty.

Thomason looked at McNulty, nodded, and turned

back towards the waiting men. "We're gonna take it. Looks to be an old couple, shouldn't be too hard. Prob'ly scare 'em to death," he chuckled as he mounted up. They pulled back from the trees and took to the roadway, intent on approaching the farm from the road, making their usual approach to demand money for taxes to support the Home Guard.

The old man, Elmer Harrigan, and his wife Myrtle, looked up at the first sound of horses coming on the hard-packed roadway. Elmer glanced at his wife, nodded to the house and she gathered her skirt about her and hastened through the front door. She grabbed up her husband's rifle, an 1851 model Sharp's carbine, and cradled her Richards double-barrel shotgun in her arms. They stood side by side in front of the house as the five men rode up.

Thomason leaned forward, "Afternoon folks. I'm Captain Thomas with the Iowa Home Guard. I've been commissioned to go around and collect taxes from the landowners to support the Home Guard. Since so many of the young men have gone to war and all the resources are used in support of the troops, we need to raise the money for the Home Guard."

Elmer frowned at the men, slowly bringing his rifle up as he spoke, "Ain't heard of no Home Guard, 'sides, ain't got no money anyway." Myrtle had followed her husband's lead and was slowly lifting her shotgun.

"Now, hold on folks," drawled Thomason as he swung a leg over the rump of his horse to step down. He stood beside his horse, one hand holding a rein, the other held up, open palmed, "We don't mean no harm but you're making my men nervous with those guns. Now, how 'bout you just set them down and we'll see what you have that will suit the Guard and we'll be on our way."

"You just git right back on that horse and skedaddle," growled Elmer, glancing from Thomason to the two men directly behind him. He noticed the last two were moving wide of the others and he spoke low to his wife, "Watch them two in the back."

Thomason nodded, slowly dropped his free hand, "Alright, alright. We'll be leavin'," and stuffed his foot in the stirrup, glanced at his men and nodded.

When the others saw his nod, they grabbed for their weapons. Cranston, the weasel, squealed as he brought up his pistol, glaring at the woman and cackling as he cocked the hammer and started to level the pistol for a shot, but the shotgun in the hands of Myrtle roared, obscuring her in a cloud of smoke, and the shot scattered and blasted Cranston clear out of his saddle, dropping him on his back behind his horse. His face and neck had been obliterated and were now nothing but a bloody mass of torn-up flesh.

But the McNulty brothers were a little faster than Elmer and their bullets took him, one in the chest, the other in the stomach, and knocked him back against the house. Denton Packard fired his rifle from the side and the bullet plowed a furrow from Myrtle's side through and through to exit her back taking a palm-sized patch of flesh with it. She was dead before she hit the ground.

The brief skirmish lasted no more than a minute but three people lay dead under the pale cloud of gun smoke. Thomason shook his head, looking at his men, "All right, Frank and Jon, you take the house, Wilbur and Dent, you take the barn.

"Wilbur's dead," growled Denton, turning toward the barn.

"What? Who shot him?"

"The woman," retorted Denton, over his shoulder.

"Figgers," growled Thomason, following the brothers into the house.

The practiced looters made quick work of the pillaging, finding a stash of coin and a few bills in a teapot on the shelf. They took the weapons and ammunition but found little else of interest to them and Thomason picked up a lantern, smashed it against the table and hollered to the brothers, "Scram! I'm lightin' her up!"

Within moments, the barn and house were ablaze, smoke starting to rise in the dusky sky. As they reined around, Jon McNulty asked, "What about Cranston?"

"What about him?" replied Thomason.

"Ain't we gonna bury him?"

"Nah, drag him over into the trees if you want. We're leavin'. You can catch up."

Jon stepped down and grabbed the body by the heels of his boots, drug him to the trees, and quickly mounted to catch the others.

The buzzards were the giveaway. Reuben had been busy digging the graves and paid little attention to the scavengers but their movement caught his eye and he straightened up to look. They were at the edge of the trees in the deep grass but something had taken their attention from the devastation at the farmhouse. Reuben dropped the shovel and walked closer, he smelled death and as he neared, he spotted the bloody body of the raider, already mauled and torn by the scavengers but certainly not a farmer.

He turned away and retrieved his shovel, looked at the two shallow graves, and jammed the shovel into the pile of dirt to return to the farmhouse. The sheriff had pulled the body of Elmer Harrigan from the rubble and had removed most of the burnt debris that covered the body of his wife, Myrtle. The sheriff looked up as Reuben returned, motioned for him to take the feet of the woman, and the two men carefully moved her body to a nearby partially burned board, then carried her from the remains of the house.

As they sat her body down, Reuben straightened,

looked at the sheriff, extended his hand, "I never said but my name's Reuben Grundy, deputy to Sheriff Thorington."

"I'm Muscatine County Sheriff, Harris Hine," replied the man, shaking hands with Reuben.

"There's another'n over yonder by the trees. I suspect he was one o' the raiders. Looks like he got blasted with a shotgun but the carrion eaters have already been pickin' at him."

The sheriff shook his head, looked from the bodies to Reuben, "You got the graves dug?"

"Two of 'em."

"Then let's get these two in the ground 'fore I get sick o' the smell."

They finished the task as quickly as possible, digging the third grave a bit shallow and were soon riding away from the farm. Before they parted, the sheriff drawled, "I signed off on this warrant for the one called Wilbur," he paused as he handed it back to Reuben, "I wish you well, don't envy you none, nosiree. If'n I had some deputies, I'd mount a posse but I figger them boys is long gone by now and outta the county. Maybe the new sheriff, don't know his name, in Iowa City'll be some help but don't count on it." Sheriff Hine gave a wave over his shoulder as he turned back east while Reuben took to the road bound to the west.

———

PEEDEE WAS NOTHING MORE THAN ANOTHER WHISTLE stop; West Liberty a little more with a few businesses but he rode past the little settlement in the dark of night. The night air had a bit of a nip to it, felt a little like frost to Reuben and he shook his head as he turned up his collar. A few miles from West Liberty, another whistle stop sat beside a water tower. One man sat on the platform before the shack, leaning his chair back on two legs, his hat over his eyes as Reuben rode up. When Reuben spoke, "Howdy!", the man dropped the chair down, shoved his hat back and sprang to his feet, looking around.

"You skeered the bejeebers outta me! What'chu doin' here, anyhow?"

"Lookin' for some men. Have you seen a bunch, maybe four or more that came through here in the last day or so?"

"What'chu want 'em fer?"

Reuben pushed his jacket back to reveal the deputy badge, glared at the man and cocked one eyebrow up as he looked at him.

"Oh, uh, yeah, there was some came through this mornin' early. Didn't say nothin but I was in the shack there. They prob'ly didn't see me, which suited me, they looked plumb mean."

"They are. They stay to the road?" asked Reuben, nodding to the roadway that passed the station house at the back.

"Ummhmm," replied the clerk.

Reuben glanced at the sun, pulled out his pocket watch and noted it to be a little aftereleven. He nudged the mule and took to the road. After leaving the sheriff to return to his office in Moscow, Reuben had ridden through the night and was tired. He planned to stop at the first place that offered cover and shade and hopefully take some food and get some rest for both him and the mules. He was gaining on the raiders and wanted to be well-rested when he caught up but he also wanted to find them before they struck again. A few miles from the station, a small clearing showed in the thicker trees and Reuben pushed his way through the underbrush to take their break.

———

HE FLIPPED THE COVER ON HIS POCKET WATCH AND WAS surprised to see it was after two. He sat up, rubbed his eyes, stood, and stretched and started to rig the mules. It had been a brief but welcome rest for both him and the mules but he wanted to make time while he could. He swung aboard Rufus, pushed through the brush and trees, and took to the road, bound to the west after the raiders. There had been few travelers on the roadway but he had passed a farmer with a wagon loaded with fresh cut lumber who was bound for West Liberty to sell the wood. Those traveling the same direction were few and far between but he had passed one man who was leisurely traveling he knew not where and was taking his time doing it. When Reuben passed him by, the smell of alcohol explained the man's lackadaisical attitude and Reuben grinned as he passed.

This was good farm country. Away from the rivers and streams, the woods were not overly thick and the land could be cleared as many already had but there was ample space for many more farms. The soil was rich and black, he had noticed that when he was digging the graves and thought it would produce fine crops. If he had a mind to farm, this would be good land but he put the idea of farming behind him when he sold the family place in Michigan. His mind had been set on seeing the western lands, land that you could travel for days and never see another human, at least that's what he had heard. But he had this to do, those who had murdered his family and burnt their homes, and others, had to be brought to justice, one way or another.

He saw a flash of yellow in the high branches of a sycamore, then heard the cry of the yellow warbler that his mother used to say was "sweet sweet sweet, sweeter than sweet". The high-pitched song was almost a squeak or a series of squeaks. He chuckled at the effort of the tiny bird to be heard, while overhead he saw the wide-spread wings of a fish hawk, or osprey, on the hunt for his meal. Reuben enjoyed riding through the woods, seeing all the creatures and birds. It was relaxing to him after the months spent hiding from the confederates and picking off their officers while hiding among the trees. Just to be able to enjoy the songbirds and watch the squirrels and more, gave him a calm he had not felt in a long time. But the thoughts of his mission brought him back and he sat tall in the saddle, shaking his head, watching the road, and searching the trees for farms and possible targets of the raiders.

He pulled the crude map from his pocket and stretched it out over his pommel. Running his finger along the railroad, he knew the roadway usually paralleled the railway and came to the village of West Liberty. Moving it further to the west, he saw the next town was Iowa City, a larger town than the others but not as big as Davenport. He lifted his eyes to look around and thought, *they'll probably hit another farm before they get to the city, so that'll be pretty soon.* He glanced at the sky; *It's gettin' 'bout time too. They usually hit just 'fore dark.* He folded the map and stuffed it back in his jacket pocket as he looked around, getting the lay of the land. It was flat here abouts, good farm country.

He nudged the mule to quicken the pace and slipped his rifle from the scabbard to check the load. The Sharps

1859 was a proven weapon in his hands but he never took it for granted. His possibles pouch, with the paper cartridges and percussion caps, hung at his side, always readily available. The rifle was loaded, the cap secure, and he slipped it back into the scabbard. He touched the butt of his Remington Army pistol, lifted it to free it from the usual leather grip that hugged the metal frame. He did not know what to expect but his training had been to stealthily approach the enemy and do it unseen and unheard. That might not be possible with this bunch.

It was when the hair at the back of his neck prickled that he paused, trusting his senses, knowing there was danger nearby. He quickly reined the mule to a stop, slowly searched the roadway before and behind, then scanned the trees. Beyond the thickets on the left, he could see cleared and harvested fields but no buildings, believing them to be further along. He nudged the mule ahead, moving slowly, as he slipped the pistol from his holster and held it before him. He breathed easy, eyes moving, listening, and the clatter of hooves on hard ground came filtered through the trees. He guessed it to be from the direction of the farm buildings and stopped. The flash of color through the trees showed movement and he nudged the mule forward again.

He heard voices, and pushed into the trees, quickly tethering the mules out of sight, and, with rifle in hand, he started picking his way through the multi-colored thickets in the direction of the sounds. Voices were raised and the sudden staccato of gunfire racketed through the trees. Reuben ran forward, moving quietly and under cover, to see that four horsemen had approached the house but now had taken cover behind a woodpile and a wagon, their horses walking away, dragging their reins. The men and were firing towards the house and, as near as Reuben could make out, there were four shooters. But smoke and the thunder of gunfire also came from the home and Reuben knew those folks needed some help.

Reuben was to the side and slightly behind the house and, although he could not see the return fire from those in the house, he could tell they were holding their own, sounded like there were at least two shooters returning fire on the attackers. But the raiders were well-experienced in their attacks and had taken protected positions for their assault.

What they had not counted on was the interference from Reuben. He was well hidden in the trees; although they were beginning to shed their leaves, the underbrush was still thick with foliage. Reuben began working his way around behind the house, often going to all fours and crawling through the brush. He was seeking a position with a better angle of fire, for he knew once he began firing, he would quickly become a target and he wanted to thin the odds a mite first. Within moments, he had traversed the rear of the house and chosen a spot at the corner of the corral adjoining the barn. He had a good angle on the man behind the woodpile and could also see the one behind the wagon but he was better protected, although exposed under the wagon box.

Reuben watched a moment, chose the furthest one behind the wagon and brought up his Sharps.

At a distance of less than a hundred yards, Reuben narrowed the sight, the blade centered on the belly of the left-handed shooter. With the back trigger, he brought the hammer to full cock, slipped his finger on the fine front trigger, and slowly squeezed off his shot. The Sharps bucked, spat smoke and lead, and the conical bullet found its mark, driving through the gut of the one known as Jon, and blasting out the back. The raider tumbled to the side, blood splattering on the wagon and pooling around his prone form, readily visible to Reuben as he lay beneath the wagon box.

Reuben's shot racketed at almost the same instant as a shot from the house and would not be easily spotted until Jon McNulty fell to the ground, prompting his brother to look around for any additional shooter. But Reuben had hidden himself well behind the corner posts of the corral as he reloaded. The firing continued from both sides but was diminishing from the house. As was his custom, Reuben sought another position and in a low crouch, scrambled around the corral and entered the barn from the rear door. A quick survey showed no others in the barn and he stealthily mounted the ladder to the loft.

He peeked over the edge of the loft, searching for any other raiders but seeing none he pulled himself up and bellied to the hay door of the upper floor. The loft was stacked with fresh cut hay, the smell strong, the hay dry. He breathed the dust and stifled a cough as he crawled to the opening. He searched the area before the farmhouse and spotted the remaining three shooters who were laying siege to the farm. One was behind the woodpile, another near the well, and the third just beyond the root cellar. Movement caught his eye and he saw the one behind the root cellar motioning to the others and guessed him to be the leader. From his vantage point, he did not have a good line of sight on the man. He chose the one behind the woodpile for his next target and slipped his Sharps forward, showing only a few inches of the muzzle of the barrel protruding from the hay door.

He waited until the man below had fired his shot and sat back to reload. He was facing the barn and as Reuben readied his shot, he purposefully pushed a handful of hay off the ledge that caught the attention of the raider. When he looked up at the loft, Reuben pulled the trigger. The bullet flew true, the target being the tobacco tag dangling from the man's pocket, driving the tag into his chest. The man, Frank McNulty, hunched over as a mouthful of blood expelled from his throat. He fell against the woodpile, kicked once, glared at the man in the loft and died.

The leader, Al Thomason, heard and saw the shot come from the hayloft, saw McNulty die, and knowing the shooter in the loft could easily pick them off, he shouted to Packard, "Let's get outta here!" motioning the last of the raiders to their horses. Reuben quickly reloaded but, when he lifted his rifle, the men had mounted and were slapping legs to their horses, hunched over their necks, and all he saw was uplifted tails and flying dirt clods.

A rifle shot came from the window of the farmhouse, gun smoke lancing into the fading light of day. Reuben was reloading as he saw the two men riding hard and fast to make their escape and he watched, looking at the crumpled bodies of the two men he shot, but neither showed sign of life. He slowly stood and descended the ladder, stepping to the open door of the barn when another rifle shot came from the house, splintering the jamb at the side of the door, inches from his head. Reuben dropped to the ground and ducked behind the door as he hollered, "Hold your fire! I'm on your side!"

The voice of a woman came from the window, "Who are you?"

"I'm Deputy Grundy from Scott County!"

"How do I know that?"

"I'll hold out my badge, just don't shoot it!" replied Reuben, shaking his head as he removed the badge from the chest of his shirt. He slowly extended the badge in hand from the frame of the doorway, "I've been after those men for a couple weeks now. They've hit several farms before this!"

"Come out and show yourself! Keep your rifle high!"

"All right! I'm coming out!" answered Reuben, slowly standing and lifting his rifle high. He stepped into the barn doorway, walking slowly toward the house. "There's two dead men here that need to be buried. Can I set my rifle down and go to work?"

"Come closer first," answered the woman.

Reuben stepped closer, rifle still raised, and asked, "Is anyone hurt inside?" But before she could answer, another shot, somewhat muffled, came from the trees near the road. Reuben unconsciously ducked and turned, expecting to see the two raiders returning, but nothing showed. He watched the roadway from his crouched position between the house and the wagon, and, after a few moments, he saw birds returning to roost in the trees, which said there was nothing out of the ordinary. He stood and turned back to the house, saw the woman standing at the door and he repeated, "Anyone hurt?"

"My father."

"Can I help?"

She pushed the door open and motioned him to enter, stepping back away from the entry. As Reuben stepped into the dim interior, he saw broken windows, holes in the walls, shattered dishes, and more. Laying on the floor, a rifle across his chest, was an older man, chest and neck bloodied, and a black-rimmed red hole in his forehead. His glassy eyes stared at the ceiling as he lay, unmoving and lifeless. Reuben looked from the corpse to the woman who was daubing her eyes with a hanky, her chest shaking with sobs. She reached for a chair behind her, sat down and buried her face in her folded arms on the table.

"Mama, can I come out now?" came a tiny voice from the crack in the door.

Reuben looked from the door to the weeping woman as she lifted her head, making an attempt at drying her eyes and wiping her nose. "Yes, dear, you can come out now." She looked at Reuben and motioned for him to cover the body of her father.

Reuben grabbed a blanket that hung near the door, obviously used to separate rooms, and quickly draped it over the body and turned his back to the prostrate form as a boy of about eight timidly walked toward his mother. The child was frowning and had not noticed the strange man but he saw his mother wiping her face, "What's the matter, mama?" and went to her side, looking up at her tear-stained face. He reached up to touch her cheek and she took his hand in hers, kissed it and held it close to her cheek. She lifted the boy to her lap and hugged him close.

Reuben spoke softly, "I'll tend to things outside first, then come in later," nodding toward the blanketed form on the floor.

"I'll not have them with my family!" she protested.

She shook her head, then dropped her eyes. "The family plot is across the road at the trees. You can put the others wherever you like but not near there." She was firm and even angry, her nostrils flaring and cheek muscles clenching as she squinted her eyes to state her will.

Reuben nodded, backing out the door, "I understand ma'am."

———

He dug one grave, in a small clearing just inside the tree line, a little wider than usual, but just as deep, sufficient for two bodies. When he had looked at the dead men, he compared their features with the descriptions he had been given and judged they were the McNulty brothers, so he thought it suitable they would be together in the grave. With a rope secured from the barn, he trussed the bodies together and went to the woods where he had tethered the mules. He pushed through the brush and trees, stopped, and looked carefully through the thicket. Where he should see the mules, he saw nothing. He drew his pistol and carefully pushed closer to the clearing, stepped into the open to see Rufus, dead on the ground. The saddle and his other gear were still secure but the pack mule and everything it carried was gone. He looked at the tracks and saw the footprints of hob-nail boots, digging in the heels and probably pulling on the recalcitrant mule. But the tracks showed the man prevailed and had mounted his horse and took off with the pack mule. Where they had been tethered was just in the trees from the road but, apparently, they had been seen from the roadway leading to and from the farm. Reuben shook his head as he looked at the dead mule, then set to work removing the saddle and other gear.

When he returned to the farmhouse, he rapped on the door. Claire, frowning, opened the door and asked, "What is it?"

"Uh, them outlaws killed my mule and stole my pack mule. I'm gonna use one of the horses to carry the bodies to the grave, then I'll come back for your father."

Claire shook her head, "Use the sorrel, the bay's too small, he's my horse."

Reuben nodded and started to the barn, his saddle over his shoulder. Within moments, he had the sorrel saddled and he led the gelding from the barn to drag the bodies of the raiders to their grave. Once there, he unceremoniously dropped them into the hole, finished shoveling the dirt over the forms, and picked up the shovel to go to the family plot.

There were two marked graves in the shady grove, *Mildred Gates Huffington, Wife and Mother, 1820-1860* and another, *Baxter Huffington, 1839-1840.* Reuben started digging a grave beside that of the woman, assuming her to be the wife of the dead man and mother of the young woman. When he finished, he stuck the shovel in the pile of dirt, used his neckerchief to wipe the sweat from his brow and neck, and led the sorrel back to the farmhouse. He went to the well and used the water in the trough to wash up, wiping the excess off with his rinsed-out neckerchief and started for the house.

He rapped lightly on the door, then pushed it open. The woman sat at the table, her son beside her, their backs to the body on the floor. Reuben glanced at the form, saw she had tended to the man and wrapped the body tightly in a different blanket. He looked at the woman, "Ma'am, I'll take the body to the grave. Do you want to say anything or . . .?"

She looked up at Reuben, "What did you say your

name was?"

"I'm Reuben Grundy, ma'am."

"And I am Claire Beckham, this is my son, Charles or Charlie."

"Ma'am," responded Reuben, nodding as he held his hat in hand. "The body, ma'am?"

"Yes, we'll be along shortly. If you would be so kind, Mr. Grundy, there are some boards in the barn that could be used for a marker, if you will."

"Yes ma'am. What would you like on the marker, ma'am?"

"Please don't use ma'am, my name is Claire."

"Yes ma'am." He raised his eyebrows in a questioning expression waiting for an answer.

"Oh, yes. The same as my mother's, the name is William, but the dates would be 1818-1862."

"Very good, ma'am, I mean, Claire," replied Reuben, turning towards the wrapped body. He bent down to hoist it to his shoulder, then carried it from the house to the waiting mule. Draping it over the saddle, he led Rufus to the family plot to bury the man.

His carving was crude but sufficient and the marker similar to that of the woman. When finished, he went to the farmhouse, knocked on the door and was surprised when the door opened and the woman and the boy, both in nicer clothes, their hair combed and slicked down, stepped out and started to the plot. As he followed, Reuben shook his head, wondering what the woman would do, now that she appeared to be alone. This was more farm than a woman alone could handle, plowing, planting and such were man's work. But he reckoned it was none of his affair. He would just see to it she and the boy were all right for now and he would be on his way, at least, that was what he thought.

13 / CHANGE

Reuben sat at the table while Claire was busy at the counter. She had insisted he stay for supper, "It's the least I can do for all you've done, Mr. Grundy," she stated as they left the grave site.

"It's Reuben, please."

She smiled at him as she navigated the trail back to the house, holding her skirt tight and lifting it above her shoes to avoid the damp weeds and more. "All right, Reuben, and you must call me Claire. After all, we've been through a war together, so we should at least use familiar names, wouldn't you say?"

"Of course, Claire. And I also wanted to talk to you about borrowing a horse to get me to Iowa City. I could make sure it gets back to you, of course."

"Let's talk about those things after we've had supper, please," she asked as they neared the door. She glanced at Reuben as he started to the well to clean up, "There's a basin and a towel on the bench beside the house," nodding to the long bench beneath the side window.

"I'll put the horse up and clean up a mite 'fore I come in," he added as he turned away.

———

As he sat at the table, he glanced at the woman at the counter. She was about his same age, maybe a year or two older, confident, and capable. She had maintained the home since her mother passed and had been well taught and schooled by her mother. Her light brown hair caught the light and shone with a reddish glow that captured his attention. He guessed her to be a little over five feet tall, well proportioned and trim, and had a pleasing face with eyes that showed intelligence and a depth not often seen in most women. She was strong and had taken the death of her father surprisingly well, but she showed her son a gentleness and love.

She had turned and was looking at him, "Reuben?" she spoke, then smiled and spoke again to the glassy eyed and thoughtful man, "Reuben?"

He glanced up at her, shook his head and smiled as his cheeks and neck showed the red of embarrassment, "I'm sorry, my mind was wandering."

She smiled, "I was asking if you wanted some fresh coffee. Supper is almost ready."

"Oh, yes, of course, please," he stumbled, straightening up in the chair.

"And just where was your mind wandering?" she asked as she stepped to the fireplace and swung the long arm with the hanging dutch oven toward her. She used the pot hook to lift the lid and stirred the stew with a long-handled spoon, replaced the lid and seated herself opposite Reuben at the table. "Supper will be ready soon, now where did your mind wander off to?"

"Well, I was wondering about you and Charlie. What will you do now?"

She dropped her eyes to the table, traced the pattern

with her finger and said, "I haven't given it much thought. But we, Pa and me, were planning to go west to join up with my Uncle Horace. He and his wife, Mildred, went with a wagon train bound for Oregon, but found a place north of Fort Kearny in Nebraska and offered to help Pa get set up in a new farm there."

Reuben frowned, "But what about this place?"

"We were struggling with the memories and we had a couple hard years. But this year, the corn crib is full, the loft is full of hay, and things were looking good, until the war. Pa had taken out a mortgage to cover the losses of the last two years and this year's harvest would have made the payments but . . ."

"It would be hard for a woman alone, especially with the likes of the ruffians and such like the ones that struck today."

"I think Pa had decided to sell out and go to Fort Kearny, he just hadn't said much."

"Do you have any other family?"

"No, my husband, Mortimer, was one of the first volunteers for the 1st Iowa Infantry. They were in several skirmishes in Missouri and were a part of General Lyon's Army of the West. My husband wrote about their exploits in saving the railroad but then marched across Missouri and were in the Battle of Wilson's Creek. His best friend, Clayborne Higel, wrote to tell me my husband was killed in that battle." She dropped her head, stifled a sob, and added, "That was just over a year ago." She stood and went to the counter, making busy to gain her composure.

Reuben let the silence reign for a few moments, then quietly explained, "When I returned home from the war, I found my family murdered and the farm burnt. I sold out, started west after those that done it, killed two of 'em today."

Claire turned, frowning, "Those same men killed your people?"

Reuben nodded silently. Breathed deeply, looked up at Claire, "I will do whatever I can to help you, whatever you decide."

"That's awfully kind of you," replied Claire, coming back to the table to touch Reuben's arm as she stood near. She looked around, went to the fireplace, and retrieved the dutch oven with the stew, sat it on the table on a wooden hot pad, returned to the fire and bent to lift the lid off a second dutch oven and scooped out some biscuits. She called to her son, "Charlie! Come to the table. We're having supper."

It was an excellent meal, pork stew with potatoes, carrots and onions, and gravy poured over the hot biscuits. The table was silent except for the rustle of plates and tableware and cups of hot coffee, fresh milk for the boy. As they finished, Reuben pushed back, stood, and took his tableware to the dish pan and returned to his seat.

With the table cleared, Claire sat down, looked at Reuben, "Pa bought a Studebaker wagon last year, was getting it ready for the trip to Fort Kearny. He was proud of it, showed me the bows, canvas, harness, and all. We have two teams of mules he used for the farm, figured they'd do the job of pulling the wagon. He had made up a list of all the things we'd need to take and such. We've got the stores, everything we'd need."

Reuben frowned, "So, you're thinking of going to Fort Kearny?"

She cocked her head to the side, lifted her eyebrows, "I

figger I could sell this place to the banker, maybe get a little extra for the crops in the barn and such. Might not get much because of the mortgage but should get a little. Don't see as I have much choice and, like you said, stayin' here doesn't seem to be the best thing. At least in Nebraska, I've got family. Maybe I can join a wagon train in Iowa City."

"Well, this time of year, I don't think you'll find any wagon train but we'll just take it one day at a time. I don't think I'm done with the raiders either. Might catch up to them in the city. But, if we're going, tomorrow's as good a time as any." He stood, pushed the chair under the table, "I'll sleep in the barn but we'll need to get an early start on loading things up."

Claire smiled, nodded, and stood. "Thank you Reuben. I'd be lost without you."

He nodded and turned away and walked out. The fading light of dusk offered ample light for him to go to the barn and he had seen a lantern that would do for the night. As he walked, he thought about Claire. She was a fine woman but he certainly had not expected to be traveling with a woman and a child. Those he pursued had already proven themselves merciless killers and not above killing women and children. But would they be any safer with him than staying alone on the farm? These were not the only border ruffians that were taking advantage of families without their men. But what else could he do? And it was not like he had any other responsibilities or family to be concerned about, and she needed help, so . . .

————

IT WAS CLOSE TO NOON WHEN THEY PULLED INTO THE edge of Iowa City. Reuben reined up the mules for a moment just to look at the busy town. It had been the first capital of the state of Iowa, but the capital had been moved to Des Moines, leaving behind a town that was struggling to recover from the loss. The University had begun to prosper and was building a new building but there were a few storefronts that were boarded up. The main street was cobblestone and the clatter of the mules' hooves followed by the rattle of trace chains and the steel-rimmed wheels caught the attention of several folks on the boardwalk. A large building on the corner sported a sign marking it as the First Bank of Iowa City and Claire said, "That's the bank. I'll need to see Mr. Claypool right away."

Reuben looked down at the four-year-old boy, Charlie, and asked, "Charlie, you wanna come with me to put the wagon and mules up at the livery?"

Charlie looked from Reuben to his mother and back at Reuben, "Ummhmm," he answered, nodding and grinning.

"Well, Claire, let me help you down and me'n Charlie will take care of the mules and be right back."

Claire smiled, waited for Reuben to wrap the lines around the brake handle and step to the ground. He reached up to give her a hand down from the spring board seat. She stepped from the edge of the wagon to the metal step, to the hub of the wheel and to the ground. Dusting herself off, she adjusted her hair, took the papers from Reuben, and started to the bank. Reuben grinned, stepped back aboard, and looked at Charlie, "Ready Charlie?"

"Ummhmm," grinned the boy, watching Reuben slap the rumps of the mules with the lines and start them toward the edge of town where the Livery waited.

As they pulled up at the big double doors of the livery, the ring of hammer on anvil echoed through the big barn. A short, stocky, man was standing before a low anvil, swinging a big hammer as he shaped a red-hot horseshoe. He poked the shoe in the fire, brought it back to the anvil and let it ring again and again. He held it up for a close look, saw the man and boy in the doorway and hung the shoe over the edge of the tub of water, and waddled toward the visitors. The man was a dwarf with the upper body of a big man. Large shoulders, upper arms, and forearms contrasted with his stubby legs, giving him the appearance of a tree stump but his broad smile made any observer look only at the man's countenance. "Howdy friends! How may I help you?"

Reuben reached out his hand to shake, "I'm Reuben Grundy, and we've got a wagon and two teams of mules and a couple horses we need to put up for the night, maybe longer. You got room?"

"I do, I do! Up until yesterday, I hadn't seen a mule in a couple months and a couple men came in with a pack mule and now you've got two teams. Only thing about mules is, I'm the only one they ever met up with that's just as stubborn as they are!" he cackled as he walked beside Reuben back toward the wagon.

"Uh, the two men that brought in the mule, what'd they look like?"

The smithy stopped and looked up at Reuben, "Why?"

"There were four of 'em that struck a farm east of here yesterday. They killed one of my mules, stole the other'n with all the packs and my gear."

"Would you recognize your mule?" asked the smithy.

"Yes, and the gear too."

"Well, let's pull your wagon through the barn, put up your animals and you can take a look see at that mule. It's in the corral out back there with the other horses. The gear's there too."

They unhitched the wagon and mules, rubbed the animals down and let the mules loose in the corral. Reuben stood on the fence and looked at the pack mule, grinning. He glanced at the smithy, "Oh, yeah. That's my mule alright. That crook in his left ear and that little white spot by his withers, that's him alright." He stepped down from the fence, "They killed my other mule, he was my rider, and the better of the two." He walked beside the smithy, leading the horses to the stalls in the barn. They would take the two next to the horses of the men that brought in the pack mule. "Where's the gear?" he asked the smithy.

"Back here in the tack room. All they did was toss it in there, the panniers, a parfleche and other stuff," answered the smithy. He walked to the tack room, opened the door, and waved Reuben to the doorway.

The room was without light except for what showed through the cracks in the wall between the siding boards

93

but it was enough for Reuben to recognize his gear, the giveaway being his frock uniform coat that was bundled atop a pannier. He nodded his head, stepping back so the smithy could close the door. "Would you know where I could find these men?"

"Prob'ly at the Four Deuces saloon. They looked to be the type and that's the only one with girls," he grinned as he laughed. "But that was yesterday when they come in, so, could be just 'bout anywhere.'"

"And where will I find the telegraph office and the sheriff's office?"

The blacksmith cackled, "Right next to one another, just past the Victoria Hotel, there on the east side of main street." He looked up at Reuben, "And that'll be two dollars for the animals an' the wagon."

Reuben counted out the coin to the smithy, thanked him, and, with Charlie by his side, started down the street. As they neared the bank, Reuben looked in the window to see Claire seated at the desk of a man, talking, and signing papers. With Charlie in hand, he walked into the bank and went to Claire's side. She glanced up, smiled, "Oh, Reuben," and pointing to the man at the desk with the quill pen, "This is Mr. Claypool. We have settled things nicely and we're almost finished."

Reuben extended his hand as the banker stood, "Pleased to meet you, Mr. Claypool." He turned to Claire, "I need to go to the telegraph office and then the sheriff's office. You might want to go to the hotel and get yourself a room. I'll be staying in the livery but I'll stop by and we'll go to supper, if that's alright?"

"Of course, Reuben. Thank you." She reached for Charlie and drew him close as Reuben tipped his hat to her and nodded to the banker, turned, and left the bank. He crossed the street to the telegraph office and quickly wrote out his report to Sheriff Thorington. *Raiders struck again, killed farmer. I killed the McNulty brothers. Last two in town here. Hope to apprehend soon.* He signed it *Deputy R. Grundy* and nodded for the clerk to send it immediately. When the clatter of the key stopped, a satisfied Reuben turned and started for the sheriff's office.

When he stepped into the sheriff's office, he was greeted by a young man, probably late teens, sporting a deputy badge that appeared tiny on his chest. He was cheerful but the size of a small mountain. He grinned broadly, held out a meaty paw and said, "Welcome stranger, how can we help you?"

"Is the sheriff in?" asked Reuben.

"Yessir, he's in his office," nodding to the closed door with the frosted glass and the sheriff's name on the glass, *Sheriff Matthew Brady.* "Is he waitin' for you?"

"No, but I need to report a killing."

"Oh, all right then, I'll fetch him," answered a now somber young deputy as he turned toward the closed door. He rapped on the door, opened it, and stepped inside. Reuben could hear the young deputy as he told the sheriff there had been a killing and the door opened wide for the sheriff and deputy to come into the outer office.

The sheriff, a man in his fifties, grey hair, clean shaven, with black piercing eyes and a confidence in his stride glared at Reuben, "You the one wantin' to report a killing?"

"That's right, sheriff," replied Reuben, extending his hand. "I'm Reuben Grundy, deputy out of Sheriff Thorington's office in Scott County." He held his jacket open to show the deputy badge.

The sheriff motioned him toward the empty desk, seating himself behind it as Reuben took the offered seat.

He noticed the big deputy remained standing beside the counter but was watching Reuben as he began his report. "I've been on the trail of these men," he lay the five warrants on the desk, pointed at one, "That one was killed by the farmer in Muscatine county, Sheriff Hine signed off on that one. These two," pushing the two on the McNulty brothers forward, "were killed when they attacked the Huffington farm this side of West Liberty. As you can see, Claire Beckham, the daughter of William Huffington, signed as a witness to their killing. There were four of them, they killed Mr. Huffington, and these two," pointing to the remaining warrants, "are in town now. They came in yesterday, put my pack mule, that they stole, in the livery."

"Sheriff," started the young deputy, "Deputy Bishop said he was talkin' to a couple men that claimed they were shot at by some guy who was trying to steal their pack mule. They said that was yesterday on the road from West Liberty."

The sheriff cocked his head to the side as he looked at Reuben, "Would that be you?"

"Oh, I did some shooting but if I shot at them, they'd be pushin' up posies 'bout now. The only shooting was when they attacked the Huffington farm and I came on the fight, joined in, and took out two of 'em," he tapped the warrants as he spoke.

The sheriff frowned, pulled the warrants closer and looked at the two unfilled warrants. He scowled as he looked at the one, leaned back and pulled open a drawer and brought out a stack of wanted posters and started shuffling through the pile. Reuben sat back, watching, and frowning, as he cocked one eyebrow up with a glance to the young deputy and back to the sheriff. Suddenly, the sheriff said, "Yup, thought so!" and pulled out a poster with a crude drawing under the name of Aloysius Thomason. He pushed it toward Reuben who leaned forward to see the poster. He grinned as he read, *Wanted for Sedition, Robbery and Murder.*

$500 reward will be paid by Clark County, Missouri, Sheriff's office. He continued to read the description of Thomason and that he and others had been Red Legs out of Missouri. They had raided across northern Missouri, southern Iowa, and eastern Kansas.

The sheriff looked at Reuben, "And that reward might be bigger by now." He paused, looking at Reuben as he thought, "You goin' after 'em?"

"Sheriff, this bunch pretended to be raising money for the Home Guard and they killed my folks, burnt the farm, and have been doin' the same across the country. I promised my brother I'd take care of our folks but I was too late. So, I'm honor bound to see this through."

The sheriff nodded, looked from Reuben to his deputy and back to Reuben, "All right then. I'll have Deputy Pratt go with you, just to keep it legal and such," he grinned as he motioned the deputy closer, "Eustis, you go with deputy Grundy here, back him up if he needs it, but let him take the lead, understand?"

"Yessir," nodded the young man. He went to the rifle rack on the wall, took down a holstered pistol and belt and strapped it on. It looked like a toy on such a big man. He grinned as he nodded to Reuben, "After you, deputy."

Reuben grinned and stood, shook hands with the sheriff and went to the door.

A s they took to the boardwalk, Reuben explained to Eustis about Claire and Charlie, "They're without any family and she thinks it best to meet up with her uncle out in Nebraska, so, if I can get things settled here, I reckon I'll be travelin' with 'em to the west. Course, I was determined to go west anyway, so . . ." he shrugged as they stepped off the boardwalk to cross an alleyway between two business buildings. Two steps brought them up to the boardwalk that lay in front of the businesses on the east side of the street. A glance ahead showed Reuben the Hotel Victoria lay just ahead and beyond the hotel was the Four Deuces saloon.

He looked at Eustis, "The smithy said he thought the two raiders would be found at the Four Deuces, what do you think?"

"Well, as my father used to say, everything seeks its own level. Whether it be water, scum, or people, and the Four Deuces attracts those of a low level, that's for sure." Reuben frowned as he looked at the young deputy thinking that was a very mature and insightful response for one so young.

"Let's stop in here at the hotel first. I would like to tell Claire that I'll be a little while before I can return for supper."

"You reckon this will just take a little while?" queried the deputy, pursing his lips as he lifted one eyebrow.

"Everything in its own time. No need to rush things," explained Reuben. The men stepped into the lobby of the hotel in time to see Claire and Charlie start up the stairs but she paused when she saw Reuben. She nodded and turned to face the deputies as Reuben explained, "I'll be going with Deputy Pratt here to see if those men are in the saloon down the street. Hopefully, we can end this here and now."

Claire frowned, "You're not going to confront them, are you? They're dangerous men, killers!"

Reuben smiled, "It needs to be done, Claire. But I'll be back in time for supper. I'll meet you in the dining room, yonder," nodding to the entry to the hotel dining room.

Claire took a deep breath, glanced to the big young deputy, forced a smile as he nodded and introduced himself.

"I'm Eustis Pratt, ma'am, pleased to meet you," he had doffed his hat as he spoke.

"I'm Claire Beckham and this is my son, Charlie. We are pleased to meet you as well, Deputy." She looked from the deputy to Reuben, and added, "I trust you will do your best to ensure Mr. Grundy returns for his supper?"

Grinning, Deputy Pratt eagerly nodded his head, finding himself, as usual, quite uncomfortable in the presence of a lady. He looked at Charlie, "And I'm pleased to meet you Charlie!" as he offered his hand to the boy. Little Charlie leaned against his mother's skirts, pulling it before him as if it were a shield.

"Then we better be going, Eustis," suggested Reuben, nodding to Claire as he turned and replaced his hat. The men walked from the lobby of the hotel without a backward glance and turned toward the saloon.

Reuben paused at the swinging doors, looking over the edge for a quick survey of the interior, then pushed into the dimly lit room. Two big windows beside the front door were all that allowed light in but, with much of the window covered with painted lettering identifying the saloon, it was little enough. It was typical of saloons and taverns in the growing towns of the territories that spawned recent states. A long bar stretched across the side wall on the left, a back bar of shelves with bottles of liquor also held a crank-operated register and rows of glasses and mugs.

Behind the bar, an aproned and balding man with more hair on his upper lip than his head nodded to the two as they stepped into the large room. Round tables with four or more chairs filled the cavernous saloon but only two tables had anyone seated. One of the tables was close to the back wall, where two men huddled together in the dim light, nursing half-empty glasses and a brown bottle without a label. One of the men glanced up as Reuben and Eustis entered but paid little attention and returned to his huddle with the other man. The other table held two old men that were carefully pacing their drinking in the darkened and cool room.

"Aye and would you gents care for a mug of ale?" asked the barkeep, grinning as he flipped the bar rag over his shoulder.

Reuben nodded and the barkeep drew two mugs of dark ale to set before the newcomers. He mindlessly grabbed his bar rag and wiped the counter to the side of the men and spoke low to Deputy Pratt, "I don't know what those two in the back are up to but they sure make me nervous."

Eustis picked up the mug before him and turned slightly toward Reuben, "You recognize those two?"

"Can't say for sure. I never saw 'em close up but, from here, they look like a good possibility." He leaned forward and raised his voice, "Say, bartender, I'm lookin' for two no-accounts that killed my mule and stole my pack mule. One of 'em calls himself Al; he's a bully and not too smart, long brown hair, 'bout six foot tall and usually dirty and smelly. The other'ns not quite as tall, black hair, a broad nose that's been broken cuz he ain't much of a fighter. He's prob'ly just as ripe as the other'n. Seen any skunks like that?"

The more Reuben talked, the more nervous the barkeep became and began inching away from him, acting busy as he wiped the bar top. When the question came, he glanced up at the Deputy, shrugged his shoulders, answered with a nervous "I dunno," and moved further away.

Reuben turned to the old men at the table near the window, "How 'bout you fellas? Seen any skunks like that around?"

One man stuttered a little as he answered, "Cain't say as I have," glancing to the two at the back table, "Course I can't see as good as I used to."

"Oh, you'd prob'ly smell these two. They'd stink of death from all the women and old men they snuck up on and shot in the back!"

The screech of chair legs on the plank floor turned everyone's eyes to the back table where the two men were rising from their seats. They casually walked toward the bar where the two deputies stood, spacing themselves out as they approached. The bigger of the two moved closer to confront Reuben and spoke, "And if we saw these men, is there a reward?"

Reuben turned toward the speaker, "Yes, there is . . ." he answered, but followed his words with a fist to the man's gut, doubling him over. Before he could straighten, Reuben snatched his pistol from the holster and almost bent the barrel over the back of the man's head, dropping him to the floor. He turned the muzzle toward the second man, Denton Packard, who was reaching for his own, but froze as his eyes flared then squinted as he looked down the barrel of Reuben's pistol, held unwavering before him.

Deputy Pratt had stepped back when Reuben dropped Al Thomason and was surprised when he stopped Denton Packard. When Reuben nodded, Eustis snatched Packard's pistol from the holster and started to step back until Reuben ordered, "Get his hide-away from his back."

Eustis' eyes widened as he stepped behind Denton and flipped up his jacket to see the hide-away pistol jammed in his belt. The deputy quickly snatched it away and moved away from the man, shaking his head as a schoolmaster would to a misbehaving child. Al Thomason was struggling to his feet, his hand at the back of his head as he stumbled, caught himself and slowly stood. Reuben had lifted Al's pistol while he was down and now watched as the man rose. He glared at Reuben who was standing with a wide grin as he looked over the barrel of his pistol. "Would you like some more?" he asked, chuckling. "If not, we'll just take a walk down to the sheriff's office and see if he might have some accommodations for you." He motioned with the pistol and as the two men started to the door, the two deputies followed close behind.

Reuben wanted to stay close to Thomason and nodded for Deputy Pratt to follow Packard as they started to the door. The door jamb was a low step above the boardwalk and Packard stepped down, flinched, and stumbled to his knees. He lifted his left hand as if to signal he was all right and came to his knees and started to stand as he turned back to face the big deputy just as he took the step, but Packard had grabbed his hideaway knife from his pantleg, and as he turned, jammed it deep into the deputy's gut. As Deputy Pratt bent over from the stabbing, Packard snarled, twisted the knife, and shoved it deep again, driving the deputy back against Thomason who fell back against Reuben. The three men crumbled into a thrashing pile as Packard turned and ran down the boardwalk.

Reuben pushed Thomason to the side, glanced down at the deputy who was struggling to hold his guts in, and got a glimpse of Packard straddling a chestnut horse and slapping legs to leave at a hard run. Reuben turned his pistol on Thomason, "Don't move! Stay where you are!" He looked up at the barkeep who stood staring, mouth agape, "Go get a doctor and the sheriff!" he shouted. He went to one knee beside Pratt, "Hold on there, don't try to move. The doctor'll be here right quick!"

"He . . .gutted . . . me!" groaned Pratt, looking at the blood oozing between his fingers. "Never . . . thought it'd . . . hap. . . pen . . . to me." He grunted, looked at Reuben with fear in his eyes, let out a slow and long breath, and lay still in death.

Reuben shook his head, glared at Thomason, thought seriously about just pulling the trigger on his pistol and finishing it right now, remembering the many burnt farms and bodies and the eager innocence of the young deputy, but the clatter of feet on the boardwalk brought him back to focus on the present.

"What happened?" growled the sheriff as he looked at Pratt then to Reuben.

"Packard had a hideaway knife, stumbled, turned and gutted the deputy," he nodded up the street, "stole a horse and took off lickety split!"

"His mama's gonna skin me alive! Never shoulda sent him with you. That was his first time outta the office. He was just s'posed to be the jailer!" The sheriff shook his head as he looked from Reuben to the street, "You goin' after him?"

"Yup. But the Beckham woman and her son will be expectin' me for supper. She'll still be around, at least till I get back, so if the reward on this'n comes in, give it to her for now. I can get my share from her later."

The sheriff nodded to Thomason, "You take him to the jail, lock him in, then you can go see your lady friend. See me 'fore you leave after the other'n."

"You're going after him?" asked Claire, incredulous.

"It's mine to do," nodded Reuben. They were at the table in the dining area of the Victoria hotel, Charlie sat beside his mother, elevated to table height with several books. Their meal had been ordered and Reuben was sipping at the hot coffee as he finished telling Claire of the day's events. "I've got to get the man 'fore he kills anymore."

"But won't he be lying in wait for you?"

"Prob'ly, or he might just be getting as far as he can as fast as he can. Either way, I'll be leaving soon," he pulled out his pocket watch, flipped it open and saw the time to be just after six. "The moon's waxin' full, so I'll have good light for tracking. He won't expect anyone coming after dark."

"Or so you think," grumbled Claire. She looked at Reuben, her gaze softening, "I know we've only known each other a few days but we've shared a lot and I feel closer to you than anyone else I know around here. I don't want to lose you too!"

Reuben was surprised at her words and did not really know how he felt about her. True, they had only known each other a few days but they had shared more in that short time than many shared in a lifetime. But he was not hankering for a double harness, at least not yet. He had decided he would do everything he could to help her and Charlie, even to taking them to Fort Kearny, but helping someone in need is not the same as . . . as what? The thoughts tumbled through his mind faster than he could put a handle on them and he stuttered to answer, "You won't be losing anything. I should be back in a couple days at most, then we can get started to Fort Kearny." He breathed deep, wondering who it was that just said all that, shook his head slightly and reached for the coffee cup to hide the embarrassment that was crawling up his neck and showing red.

―――――

THE BIG MOON GLOWED SILVER AS IT HUNG HIGH IN THE eastern sky. The leaves that in the daylight showed so many brilliant hues of red, orange and gold, now shimmered with shafts of silver chased by dark shadows. The night sounds of loons came from some nearby pond and nighthawks circles overhead, sounding off with their occasional *pee-yah* or the sharp squealing chirp. The shuffling gait of the blaze-faced sorrel beneath Reuben made little sound on the dusty and leaf-strewn roadway.

When Packard had left town at a dead run, the clatter of hooves on the cobblestones caught everyone's attention and Reuben had little difficulty getting bystanders to tell him which road the fleeing man chose. When the running horse hit the dirt road, he left tracks that could be followed by a half-blind granny, even in the moonlight. But the horse had soon slowed and now the roadway was little help in showing Reuben where Packard had fled.

Reuben tried to put himself in Packard's frame of mind, considering what he would do if he were the man who was literally running for his life. He knew Packard had no weapons, save the hideaway knife, unless there was a rifle in the ever-present scabbard with most saddles. But without a weapon, that would be the first thing the man would want to lay hold of, that and food, perhaps extra clothing. So, what would he do? If he met up with a traveler, he would probably waylay him, but if not, he would search out a common target, a farmhouse.

The quiet of the night was suddenly shattered by the

boom of a rifle, followed closely by another. A scream that rivaled that of a wounded bobcat split the darkness and Reuben dug heels to the ribs of the sorrel, searching for a roadway that would take them in the direction of the commotion. He lay low on the sorrel's neck, mane slapping his face, yet he reached for the Sharps and withdrew it from the scabbard to lay it across the pommel. Without missing a step, the sorrel followed his lead as he leaned to the left to take the cut-off road that cut through the nearly naked trees. A light shown through the window of a small farmhouse, shadowy figures before it, as Reuben slowed the sorrel in his approach. "Hello the farm! I'm comin' in and I'm a deputy sheriff!" he shouted, nudging the sorrel forward. As he moved, he brought the Sharps to full cock, keeping his fingers on the trigger guard, but ready to swing the barrel and take a shot if need be. He saw a shirtless man standing in the doorway, braces over his shoulders that held up his britches, barefoot on the cold ground. Cradled in his arms was a Richards double-barreled shotgun, hammers cocked and his finger on the trigger as it slowly lifted toward Reuben.

On the ground, the still form of Packard was being tended to by a woman in a long nightshirt, kneeling on the far side of the man and daubing at blood on the man's chest and neck. He had taken at least one barrel of buckshot, perhaps more. Reuben looked up at the farmer, "I've been on that man's trail. He escaped from town this afternoon. He's one of a bunch that was claiming to be Home Guard and were looting farms and killin' folks."

"He ain't gonna kill nobody else, mister," came the voice of the woman as she struggled to her feet. "He's plumb dead!" She looked at her man, shook her head and started to the house. The man looked at Reuben, "I heard somethin' out here, thought it was a coyote after the chickens. When I came out the door, I saw him comin' from the barn. When I hollered, he shot, an' when he shot, I let go with ol' Betsy here," patting the shotgun. "Can't miss with Betsy."

"Don't look like," replied Reuben. "Did you see his horse anywhere?"

"I think it's back 'side the barn yonder." He looked from Reuben to the body, "You takin' this with you?" motioning to the form at his feet.

"Prob'ly. Sheriff needs to know 'bout it."

Reuben rode to the barn, leaned down and untied the rein of the stolen horse, led it back to the farmhouse and stepped down. He looked at the bloody mess at his feet, looked up at the farmer, "Give me a hand?"

The farmer grunted, sat the shotgun by the door, and helped Reuben load the dead body of Denton Packard. Reuben strapped it down and thanked the farmer, mounted up and led the chestnut behind as he rode down the dark roadway.

The big moon rested on the dark treetops in the west behind him when Reuben rode back into Iowa City. As he rode down the main street, the horses' hooves clattered on the cobblestones, prompting some lamps to be lit as he rode down the street. He guessed it to be pushing five o'clock in the morning as he reined up in front of the sheriff's office and jail. He breathed deep, slid from his saddle, and slapped the reins over the hitchrail, mounted the boardwalk and pushed through the door of the office. A low burning lamp sat on the counter, while behind the desk, a deputy dropped his feet to the floor and sat upright, shaking his head as he looked at the tired figure before him. He frowned,

"Who're you, an' what'chu want at this time o' mornin'?" he growled.

"I'm Deputy Reuben Grundy. Sheriff Brady's expectin' me to bring in a prisoner but I got a body instead."

The grumpy deputy scowled, "Where?"

"Out front on a horse."

"What timesit?"

Reuben shook his head slowly, looked at the wall clock with the swinging pendulum, "That says it's a little after five!"

The man rubbed his eyes, looked up at Reuben, "You're the one that was with Eustis when he got gutted, ain'tchu?"

"Ummhmm, and the one that dunnit is on the horse out there," nodding over his shoulder to the front of the office.

"Well, sit down. I'll put on some fresh coffee."

"Nope. I'll tend to my horse at the livery, then come back for that coffee. I'll leave the package there," he nodded and turned away to walk outside.

The smithy was already busy stoking up his fire and feeding the animals when Reuben rode into the big barn. He stepped down, led the sorrel into a stall and grabbed a handful of hay to rub the horse down. When he turned back, the smithy stood with a bucket of grain in one hand, a bucket of water in the other. He handed them off to Reuben, nodded, and went back to his work.

The coffee was strong and hot, and Reuben had no sooner sat down than the front slammed open and Sheriff Brady strode in looking like a bull on the prod. He hollered at his deputy, "What's that horse and dead man doin' out there?"

"Not much of nuthin', Sheriff," drawled the deputy.

He nodded toward Reuben who sat in the shadows beyond the pot belly stove. The Sheriff recognized Reuben when he leaned into the light, "That the one you went after?"

"That's him, but I didn't do that. He tried stealin' from the wrong farmer and got a load of buckshot for his efforts."

"Good, good. Well, that does it, don't it?"

"He's the last, 'cept for the one you got back there."

"Yeah, well he won't be there long, the judge'll be here in a day or two. That woman of yours gave me a sworn statement, identified him too. So, it'll go quick. Judge Blackburn'll hang him, shore. I'll be sendin' a telegram to that sheriff in Missouri to get your reward, it usually only takes a day or so for the banks to agree and this'n here'll pay out."

––––––––

REUBEN STOOD, STRETCHED, "I WAS GOIN' TO SLEEP IN THE livery but since the sun's up and he'll be playin' a tune on that anvil, I think I'll get me a room at the hotel. Maybe get me some breakfast 'fore I hit the sack. Mrs. Beckham wants to get started for Fort Kearny soon, so the sooner that reward comes in, the better."

"I'll see to it you get it soon's it comes in," grumbled the sheriff as he started for his office.

Reuben pulled his hat down and walked outside, glanced at the rising sun and the waking town, and went to the hotel for a meal and a bed. He was anxious for both but, first, he needed the breakfast. Maybe he'd see Claire before he turned in for some sleep; hopefully, she'd understand the delay.

Sheriff Thorington –

Last of Home Guard captured. Aloysius Thomason in custody Iowa City Sheriff Brady. Denton Packard killed by farmer. Leaving deputy badge with Brady. Thanks.

Reuben Grundy

Reuben pushed the written gram to the telegraph operator and asked, "How much?" The operator counted the words, calculated and looked up at Reuben, "You can send this collect to the sheriff, if you want, otherwise it'll be five dollars an' forty cents."

Reuben grinned, "Send it collect. I've paid enough." He stayed long enough to see it sent, got an acknowledgment it was received, and left the telegrapher's office, bound for the nearby emporium. A quick stop saw him pick up some writing paper, an envelope, and a pencil and with a nod, left to return to the hotel.

A wave from Claire beckoned him to her table where

she sat with a squirming Charlie. She smiled as he seated himself, "So, you got your telegram sent?"

"I did and picked up some writing material so I can send a letter to my sister."

"I'm sure she will be glad and probably relieved to hear from you."

"She's all the family I have left. It was hard to leave but she understood. I'm just not cut out for farming and I wanted to get as far from the war as possible." The last words dropped off as he lowered his gaze and looked at the table of fare for the dining room. The waitress had already brought him a cup of coffee and was returning to take his order.

"The special will be fine," he stated, dismissing the waitress, then looked at Claire. "The sheriff said he should hear back on the reward today and, if it goes as he expects, the bank should pay the funds today or tomorrow at the latest."

"That's good to hear. You deserve it for all you've done. Why, if it weren't for you, those outlaws would still be raiding and killing more innocent farmers and who knows what all!"

"But, I figger to share it with you," stated Reuben, frowning.

"Oh no! I did nothing but defend our home and, if you hadn't come, I would probably be in a grave beside my Mom and Dad. No, no, I'm fine. The money from the farm and the harvest and stock, is quite sufficient to see me through whatever may come."

"You sold the harvest and crops?"

"Ummhmmm, the banker was kind enough to include those in the settlement. He said he knew a neighboring farmer that would be glad to get the stock and the local feed store would take the corn, wheat and hay."

"That was mighty kind of him."

"Oh, it was convenient for me, and I'm certain the banker will make a profit on everything. He didn't think I knew much about crop prices and such but I upped the ante on him and got a fair price, considering." She smiled coyly as she straightened the tableware before her.

"Remind me to never to play cards with you!" chuckled Reuben. He grinned at Claire, looked at Charlie who had found the linen napkin and was playing quietly. "I reckon that as soon as the bank settles up on the reward, we can start for Fort Kearny. I was talking with the smithy about the route to the Fort; he's talked with several travelers goin' both ways and he said that by wagon, it's about a month's journey, give or take. That would put us the end of October, first of November gettin' in there. If you send a telegram or a letter, which'll go by rail and maybe stage or Pony Express, your uncle will have time to make arrangements and such."

"Then I guess we'll both be writing letters!" she declared, smiling broadly as she glanced to see the waitress returning, arms full of plates of food. They both leaned back for the woman to set the table, thanked her and just as Reuben grabbed a fork, Claire gave him a look that stopped him as she added, "We must say grace first, Reuben. We must always be thankful for what the Lord has done for us, don't you agree?"

"Uh, yes, I reckon," he mumbled as he bowed his head. He glanced up to see her looking and waiting, "Me?"

"Haven't you ever asked the Lord's blessing before?"

"Uh, well, uh, yeah, I guess so, but it's been so long, maybe you better."

Claire smiled, lowered her head, and quietly said a

brief prayer of thanks, then lifted her smiling face as she said, "Umm, smells good!" and began eating.

———

"WHAT'S THAT?" ASKED REUBEN. HE WAS GAWKING AT THE store clerk as he placed two new rifles in the wall rack behind the counter. What he saw was something different than anything he had seen before and it piqued his curiosity. Always being a man interested in firearms, especially after his stint in the Sharpshooters, rifles held a special interest for him.

The clerk chuckled as he turned, holding a rifle across his chest, "Ain't it a beauty? It's the new Henry Repeater. Comp'ny's trying to get the army to buy 'em but they're holding back for some reason. The salesman said some o' the generals think the troops would waste too much ammunition!"

Reuben frowned, stretched out his arms to hold the rifle offered by the clerk. It was smaller and lighter than his Sharps, had a brass mounted receiver and fittings, and looked more like a show piece than anything he had seen before. "You said 'repeater'?"

"That's right," he turned to pick up a copper cartridge and offered it to Reuben. "Takes these cartridges, loads fifteen of 'em," he pointed to the tube beneath the barrel, "and as fast as you can pull the trigger, and cock that lever, it'll load 'em for you and all you gotta do is pull the trigger!"

Reuben frowned, looking from the clerk to the rifle and back again, thinking the clerk was joshing him. He lifted the weapon to his shoulder, sighted down the barrel, lowered it and cocked the lever, watching the mechanics of the weapon. "Fifteen, you say?"

"That's right. We got five of those in, company wants to get some folks used to 'em, maybe buy 'em for their boys in the army."

"What about the cartridges, got plenty?"

"Couple cases, more comin'," nodded the clerk.

"How much?" asked Reuben, thinking about the reward money and how this rifle would be an asset as he traveled with the woman and boy.

"Forty dollars. That'll get you one box o' cartridges with it."

Reuben frowned, "That's more'n a month's wages for most folks!"

"Can't draw wages if you're dead!" retorted the clerk. He was an older man, walked with a limp and Reuben knew right off the man had probably wanted to join up but the army would not take him.

Reuben thought a moment, hefted the rifle, lifted it to his shoulder and sighted again, then lowered it and said, "Add it to the rest of the stuff." All they needed was some more staples, flour, sugar, salt, some smoked pork belly, corn meal, and cartridges and powder and lead for his rifle and pistol. "Add five, no, six boxes of cartridges for that rifle. What'd you call it?"

"Henry Repeater, .44 caliber."

He looked at Claire as she fingered some cloth, stepped near, "If you want it, get it. It'll be a while 'fore we stop at a store like this and be sure to get extra clothes and boots for Charlie." He chuckled, "And be sure to get some of that penny candy for the boy."

Reuben watched the clerk as he tallied everything up, smiling at the good sale. He looked up at Reuben, gave him the total and Reuben counted out the new greenbacks, eliciting another smile from the clerk. Reuben asked, "You know much about the roads and trails goin' west from here?"

The clerk slowly shook his head, "No sir, I'm afraid I don't. Once I opened this store, I don't think I've been more'n ten miles in any direction. Came from Pennsylvania, I did, but that was nigh unto twenty year ago, town was just a little place then. Started by Governor Lucas, he wanted the capital near the center of the territory, now they went an' moved it to Des Moines!" He shook his head as he finished stacking the goods on the counter.

"Who would know? We're headin' west to Fort Kearny, and 'bout all we know for sure is it's west!" chuckled Reuben.

"Talk to the smithy. Before he settled down, he had been all over, trapping and such, and he knows most places and how to get there. What he doesn't know by experience, he'll know because he talks to everyone that comes in and learns 'bout things thataway. I think he misses his own travels."

Reuben nodded, "I'll be back for this," putting his hand on the stack of goods, "in a short while. Gotta go to the livery and get our wagon."

The clerk nodded, pushed the stack to the side, and turned to finish his stocking of the rifles and more. Reuben went to Claire's side, "You and Charlie should go to the dining room while I go get the wagon. I'll join you as soon as it's loaded and we'll have a good meal 'fore we take to the road."

Claire smiled and nodded, took Charlie's hand, and started to the hotel while Reuben started for the livery. He strode to the distant sound of hammer on anvil and, within moments, he walked through the big double doors of the livery. The smithy looked up from the forge, nodded, and continued his work while Reuben caught up the mules and horses, harnessed the teams and hooked up the wagon. A once over check of all the trace chains, single trees, double trees, harnesses and more, and he was ready to leave.

He walked close to the smithy, stepped in front of him to catch his eye and when he stopped his swing, Reuben said, "Need to settle up but, first, I need some directions. We're headin' to Fort Kearny, and I know it's on the Platte River in Nebraska territory, and I hear you're a travelin' man, so what do you think is the best way from here?" He watched as the little man placed the hammer on the anvil, stretched by leaning backwards, hands on his hips, then leaned against the end of the anvil and started to speak but Reuben stopped him by asking, "What is your name, anyway?" frowning with a hint of a smile.

"My full name is Alexander Thermopolai Nacadoches, so, you see why I answer better to Smithy!"

Reuben chuckled, nodding, and upended a nearby bucket and looked at the smithy, waiting for his directions.

The smithy smiled, "Yes, I was a travelin' man, been most ever place there is to go within a month's ride in any direction and if I was goin' to Fort Kearny, and since you're in a wagon, there's two ways to consider. The first would be to take that road yonder," nodding out the door to the left of the livery and a well-traveled road. "That will take you to Marengo, Newton, and on to Des Moines and beyond. All good road, easy goin' for a wagon. The other way, cross country, not so easy on a wagon and if I was alone and horseback, I'd go that way. It bears southwest to Oskaloosa and Osceola and is shorter. And of course, the railroad's been surveyin' and clearin' some o' the land thataway, and there's more roads an' trails there since I been down there."

"But I'm not alone and on horseback, so, you think we could do it with a wagon?"

"Prob'ly, an' it would save you some miles an' time, that's for sure."

"Well, the sooner I get shuck o' the wagon and the woman, the sooner'll I'll be on my own and back on track for the western country," surmised Reuben.

"Ummhmmm, and a word to the wise. There's always highwaymen to watch for, especially since you're one man with a woman. If I was you, I'd be horseback beside or in front of the wagon. And I've heard tell of some o' them Jayhawkers outta Kansas and Bushwhackers outta Missouri that have been raidin' this far north, so don't be too trustin'. If you can, and are wantin' to, you might join up with others goin' west, cuz with the war, there's plenty of pilgrims and copperheads gettin' shuck of this country and the war."

"Copperheads?" asked Reuben.

"Ummhmm, it's what some folks are callin' those that are agin' slavery but more agin' the war. Think we should just talk things over and quit killin' each other. Most of 'em are politicians, democrats!" he spat the word, "But not all democrats are copperheads; 'sides they ain't the ones you gotta worry 'bout; it's them others tryin' to force their way on folks and thievin' and killin' while they're doin' it!"

Reuben stood, shook hands with the smithy, and went to the wagon. *And here I thought it was all over with when the last of the Home Guard was done. Guess it's gonna be something to be watchful about from here on out. Maybe it'll be better further west,* he mused as he mounted the spring seat of the wagon. With a slap of the reins, the mules leaned into their traces and the wagon emerged from the livery. The sun was high above and warming Reuben's shoulders as he sighed heavily, heading for the emporium to pick up their supplies. *Well, at least we'll have us a good meal 'fore we leave.*

The bushy tailed fox squirrel sat on the oak branch, scolding the passersby in the wagon. Little Charlie pointed him out, "Look momma, that'ns got a biiig tail!" laughing as he listened to the chorus of the woods. On the ground beside the big oak, a pair of chipmunks were stuffing their cheeks full of acorns and scampering about hurriedly preparing for winter. Further back in the trees, they saw a porcupine waddling away, his spiny quills accenting his waddle. Charlie looked at Reuben who sat on the far side of Claire, both hands full of reins for the four mules. He had sold his pack mule to the smithy, taking most in trade for shoeing the mules and two horses, and the two horses trailed behind the wagon. "Reuben, are porkypines good to eat?"

Reuben chuckled, "Dunno Charlie, never had the hankerin' to find out. Those quills he carries ain't for show, you know. You get some o' those stuck in you, they're mighty hard to get out an' if you don't get 'em out, they start to fester and hurt awful bad!"

"Yeah, prob'ly," replied Charlie, searching the trees and bushes for any other animals of interest. He pointed out a bunny that sat at the side of the road just before a Harrier swooped low and snatched the little fur ball from the ground and lifted it aloft to disappear over the tree tops.

"Wow! What was that?"

"That was an owl," replied his mother.

"Nope, that was a harrier. Looks like an owl but white rump and black wingtips are the difference," informed Reuben, casual in his correction but wanting the boy to know the difference.

Claire looked from Reuben to Charlie, "So, now you know, Charlie."

"Do they sound like an owl, Reuben?" asked Charlie, leaning forward to look past his mother.

"No, their call is a high-pitched repeated squeal, kind of like a shrill whistle and sometimes a quick repeated chirp."

"Can you make that sound?"

Reuben grinned and attempted to mock the harrier, much to the delight and laughter of all three.

The terrain was a mix of hardwood and pine forests to lazy rolling plains. Several farms sided the roadway with harvested fields and homes that varied from dugouts to clapboard structures and barns from lean-tos to hip-roofed two stories. The roadway showed signs of the railroad crew making way for the coming railroad but there was much to be done before real construction could begin. Stakes and ribbons marked the surveyed right-of-way that sometimes cut across the corners of farmers' fields and even intersected the roadway. While the road twisted and turned because of the terrain, the surveyed railway was straight as the flight of an arrow.

After leaving Iowa City, they crossed the shallow Old Man's Creek, and had made good time. The mules were anxious to stretch their legs and eagerly put the miles behind them. There had been little sign of civilization, save the scattered farms. Only one sign showed a village near the roadway and they had passed no one on the road since they left Iowa City. The sun was lowering to the tree tops before them where a long line of faded colors showed the many trees that still clung to the few leaves that had not fallen prey to the cold nights and fall breezes. "Looks like a good place to make camp for the night," suggested Reuben, nodding to the tree line.

Claire smiled, then frowned, "Looks like someone else had the same idea," pointing to a whisper-thin line of smoke that rose from the trees.

"Hmmm, we'll hafta be a mite cautious," started Reuben, looking at Claire. "Say, you have your weapons handy?"

Claire smiled, "My pa's Colt Revolving shotgun is right behind me and my Paterson Colt is in my handbag beside me."

"Both loaded?"

"Of course. My pa always said, 'a gun that ain't loaded ain't no good!' and he made certain that I always knew that and he taught me how to use them." She chuckled at the thought, "But I will admit, that shotgun scares me a mite."

"Can't blame you on that score, for sure. Those things are almost as dangerous to the shooter as they are to the target," replied Reuben. He glanced beside his left leg at the new Henry and touched his Remington Army revolver that was nestled in the holster at his left hip, butt toward his right side, with his elbow, just for reassurance. He was remembering the admonitions of the smithy about highwaymen and the Bushwhackers and Red Legs.

As they neared the tree line they caught a glimpse of a cookfire and some shadows passing in front of the light, so Reuben intentionally looked for an opening or clearing on the opposite side of the roadway yet near the riverbank. He had quizzed the smithy for all the possible details he could remember about this country and he supposed the river beyond the trees was the English River, or a fork of it at least. Within a short distance, a clearing offered a good site and there was evidence of it being used before. The remains of a fire ring, three logs for seats framed the fire ring, some stacked firewood, and some dried and scattered horse apples all showed the site had seen considerable use. Reuben pulled the mules to a stop, tied off the reins to the brake lever and jumped to the ground to help Charlie and Claire.

While Reuben tended to the animals, stripping their harness, taking them to water, rubbing them down, Claire and Charlie set to work with the cookfire and supper. The setting sun sent fingers of red and orange clawing at the underbellies of the clouds as the sky shouldered the robes of dusk. Charlie was running around the campsite, trying to look and sound like the harrier, and constantly exploring the new surroundings, while Claire cautioned, "You stay close now, y'hear Charlie?"

"Yes'm, I will," but he slowed down nary a bit.

Reuben glanced his way, shaking his head and smiling at the energy of the youngster, as he busied himself rubbing down the last of the mules that stretched out and arched his back under the delightful feel of the handful of dry grass in Reuben's hands. The mule sawed back and forth, shook his head, and groaned, showing his pleasure with the rubdown. Reuben's attention was all on the mule and was surprised when Claire called, "Charlie! Charlie! Where are you son?"

Reuben looked toward Claire, then quickly looked where he saw Charlie last, and the boy was gone. He dropped the grass and stepped quickly to Claire's side. She looked at Reuben, fear showing in her eyes, "Have you seen him?" she asked, frantically, visually searching the trees and brush.

"He was right there just a moment ago," said Reuben, nodding to a serviceberry bush, heavy with fruit. "Maybe he's looking for more berries," offered Reuben. But just as he started toward the trees, Charlie came bounding from the brush, followed closely by another boy, a colored boy.

"Hey Ma! Look! I found a new friend! This is Amos!" declared the happy youngster, motioning at the boy to come close. The boy appeared to be about the same age, maybe a little older than Charlie, but he looked at the ground, head down, timidly coming near. He glanced up at Claire who smiled and said, "Well, hello, Amos. Is that your camp, yonder?"

"Yes'm, that's our camp," he replied. The boy was wearing only his britches, held up with one strap angled over the opposite shoulder and stood barefoot beside Charlie.

"Have you been here long, Amos?" asked Claire.

"No ma'am. We just stopped a while ago. It's my fam'bly, my ma, pa, sister Liza, and little brother, Andrew."

"Well, you must be proud of such a big family." She looked to Reuben, "This is Reuben, I'm Claire, and you've already met Charlie."

Before he could respond, a man pushed through the

brush, stopped, and looked around, "Amos, boy, I tol' you to stay close! What'chu doin' botherin' these folks?"

"Oh, he's no bother. I was just going to invite him to stay for supper. Have you folks eaten yet?"

"Uh, no ma'am, my missus is fixin' supper now."

"Well, since we're neighbors, perhaps your missus would like to combine our meals and have it together, what say?"

The man frowned, looked from Claire to Reuben and the boy, then back to Claire, "Uh, I don't know, ain't never had no invitation like that afore."

"Well, you tell your missus I'm fixing a mess of pork chops, potatoes and gravy, and if she'd like to put it all together, just bring it on over and we'll have us a get-acquainted get together!" She smiled broadly, saw the surprised expression on the man's face, then frowned as she added, "Go on now, but hurry back 'fore the food gets cold!"

The man nodded, motioned to his son, and they both pushed through the brush and disappeared. Reuben chuckled, walked closer to Claire, grinning at her, "You just can't help yourself, can you?"

"What do you mean?" she asked, frowning and genuinely perplexed.

"Every time you get a chance to order a man around, you just can't help yourself."

Claire smiled, laughing, and turned back to the fire to finish preparing the supper.

I t was an awkward time for a spell, but everyone seemed to grow more comfortable the longer they talked. The most talkative of the group was Claire who seemed to be starved for the companionship of a woman but the men sat back listening and adding tidbits of comment every now and again. Once the meal was over, Reuben motioned for the man, Eli, to join him for a walk about away from the women and youngsters. Relationships between coloreds and whites were tenuous at best, differing with the times, locales, and people. With the war waging further east and the impact and effects of the fighting spreading across the land, everyone was cautious in all relationships, conversations, and gatherings.

As the men started away, Eli remarked, "So, you served with the north?"

"That's right, Berdan's Sharpshooters. But I had enough of killing to last more'n a lifetime, so when my hitch was up and I was to be mustered out because of my wounds, I jumped at the chance and lit a shuck outta there!" he chuckled as he remembered the first days out

126

of uniform. He glanced at Eli, "I don't mean to be nosy, Eli, and if you think I am just tell me, but I was wonderin' if you folks are travelin' far?"

"Don't rightly know. I heard tell of free land out west and I've always been good with my hands at carpentering and at farming, so I thought it might be a chance to put all this war stuff behind us and get a little place of our own."

"So, I take it you're freeborn?"

"That's right, an' my missus was given her manumission papers when she was just a young girl, her an' her mammy both. It were a business man in Philadelphia, he died and his missus set all their slaves free. Then she put my missus and her mammy back to work in the house like they done afore, only paid 'em a wage an' such." He chuckled as he remembered, "I worked for a carpenter and we was building a barn for the business man 'fore he died, and I saw my missus then, an' ever chance I got after that, we saw each other until finally we got ourselves hitched!" He cackled, shaking his head, "And 'fore we knowed it, we had us a whole family of chilluns! Then when all this war stuff broke out, I thought 'bout joinin' up but there weren't no one to take care o' my family, so . . . here we be."

They stood on the bank of the river, enjoying the sounds of water, bullfrogs, and somewhere further away, the low hoot of loons. Reuben sat down in the grass, watching the fading light bounce off the ripples, "I'm taking Claire and Charlie to Fort Kearny. Her uncle has a farm near there and offered Claire and her dad his help in getting them set up in a place of their own, so after her pa was killed, she decided to take him up on his offer."

"Ain't she your wife?" asked Eli, puzzled.

Reuben chuckled, "Oh no, we're not married. I'm just helping her out. I was there when her pa was killed and she didn't want to stay on her farm, and I was plannin' on goin' west, so . . ."

"Well, I'll be jiggered! I thought the two of you were married! So, you're just helping them get to Fort Kearny?"

Reuben nodded, tossed a small rock across the still water, watching it make three skips. The ripples spread but soon faded with the slow-moving current. A lonesome owl asked his questions of the night and a night hawk let a short screech scratch the fading sky. Reuben looked at Eli, "So, I guess what I'm asking is if you want to travel together?"

"You sure?"

"Yup, I'm sure. I think it'd be safer for all of us."

"Safer?"

"Ummhmm. Haven't you heard about the Bushwhackers and Red Legs?"

"Yeah, but I didn't think they were up here. Thought they were down in Missouri and Kansas."

"Mostly, but they've also been raiding north. And there are those that use the war as an excuse to make raids on unsuspecting folks. I chased a bunch that called themselves the Home Guard, but the only thing they guarded was their own loot from raiding and killing innocent folks."

They sat quietly a few moments until Eli turned to Reuben, "So, how long you think it'll take us to get to Fort Kearny?"

Reuben grinned, "Bout a month, give or take."

"So, we could lay up there through the winter, get an early start come spring?"

"Sounds reasonable," answered Reuben, grinning as he offered his hand to Eli to shake on the agreement.

Breakfast was fried cornpone and black coffee at the cookfire in the Carpenter camp. The sun was barely showing its face with gold lances stretching into the retreating darkness when the two wagons lined out, Claire driving hers in the lead while Reuben was mounted on the sorrel. They forded the shallows of the English River without incident and were soon dripping dry as they pushed from the woods into the open plains of the flats. The Carpenter wagon was a farm wagon sans bows but the cargo was covered with a canvas. Eli drove with his wife, Martha, at his side, the children settled atop the canvas. A sturdy pair of mules were in harness and showed little effort with their task, and another mule trailed behind.

Reuben ranged a mile or so ahead, watchful for anything that would present a hazard, whether nature or outlaw. He had thought about taking some time out and unlimbering the new Henry rifle when a white tail buck sprang from a low brush-covered depression and bounded toward a distant thicket. Reuben slipped the Henry from the scabbard, jacked a shell into the chamber and brought it up to a quick sight on the whitetail, and squeezed off his shot. But the sorrel was startled and sprung to the side, almost unseating Reuben. The gelding dropped his head between his front feet, stretched out, kicked at the clouds with his back feet and bent in half twisting in the middle. Reuben grabbed leather and mane, struggled to hold onto the Henry, and started praying. Suddenly the sorrel tried sunfishing, showing his belly to the sky and drove his front feet into the ground. And that was just the beginning. The horse

129

bucked, kicked, tossed his head, twisted, and reared up pawing at the sun, doing everything he could to lose his rider, but Reuben clung tightly with legs, toes, arms, and hands. When the horse took off at a run, his rider laying low on his neck, he headed for the trees. Reuben looked up through the slapping mane, saw the trees coming fast, reached behind him and jammed the Henry home in the scabbard, then drove his feet deep in the stirrups, sat up and reared back on the reins, pulling the sorrel's head up and with all his might, he pulled the horse's head to the side, forcing the animal into a circle, until the horse stood spread-legged, winded, sides heaving and head down.

Reuben breathed deep, kept a taut grip on the reins, and reached down to stroke the neck of the sorrel, speaking softly to settle him down. In a few moments, Reuben felt the horse begin to relax and he slowly gave slack to the rein. When the horse shifted his weight, brought his legs under him, and stood, shaking, and breathing heavy, Reuben slowly stepped down, stood before the horse stroking his head, ears, and neck, talking all the while. He saw a line of trees and brush that promised a creek and began walking toward the thickets, leading the sorrel behind him. Once at the creek, he loosened the girth on the saddle, let the sorrel take a drink and pulled him back as he knelt close and scooped up a handful for himself. He led the sorrel around in a circle, settling him down, then let him have another drink.

He started back to the road, remembered the deer, and started looking around for the carcass. He was certain he had scored a hit and his search soon yielded a find. He chuckled, rubbed the neck of the sorrel, spoke softly to him. "All right, I won't shoot from the saddle again, if I can help it. But you need to be ready for that, cuz there might come a time when I don't have a choice. So, we might have to practice that a mite, ya reckon?" The gelding looked at him like he understood and Reuben went to work on the deer.

In short order, he had the buck field dressed and draped across the rump of the sorrel. He mounted up, sitting easily in the saddle and started the sorrel toward the wagons. The horse acted as if nothing had happened, and when they rode close, Claire asked, "What have you done to that horse?" nodding to the lather under the edge of the saddle blankets, his tail and on his chest.

"Aw, we just got a little exercise. I'll tell you 'bout it over supper." He dropped the carcass into the back of the wagon, stepped down and stripped the gear from the horse, gave him a good rubdown with a handful of dry grass and soon mounted the spring seat and took the reins to give Claire a break. She looked at him with a sidelong glare, frowning, and said, "We should make camp pretty soon. It'll take a while to cut that up," nodding to the back of the wagon and the deer carcass.

"Ummhmmm," answered Reuben, letting a bit of a smile split his face.

The south fork of the Skunk River was much the same as the north fork, wide and shallow, gravelly bottom, and easy crossing. They had crossed the north fork just after breakfast and were planning their mid-day stop before crossing the south fork but chose to cross first, rest later. The low rolling flats and good road allowed the two wagons to make good time. After crossing the north fork, they passed a sign with arrows showing the turn-off to Rose Hill and the road to Oskaloosa that showed it to be ten miles further. Reuben guessed they had covered close to five miles since the turn-off and once across the river, another five miles would see them into Oskaloosa.

The road between the forks had flanked a trio of timbered hills before coming to the banks of the south fork and once across, Reuben waved the wagons into the thin trees and grassy flats on the south side of the road for their late mid-day break. As soon as the wagon drew to a stop, Claire dropped her elbows to her knees, cradled her head in her hands and breathed deep.

"What's the matter, wore out are ya?" asked Reuben as he moved the sorrel alongside the wagon.

She lifted her head and looked at him, shaking her head, "Yes, I'm wore out! Two river crossings and this is the first stop we've made! Is this what it's going to be like all the way to Fort Kearny?" she asked, somewhat flustered.

Reuben smiled, shook his head as he stepped to the ground and raised his hand to help Claire to the ground, "Nah, this is nothin'! The further we go, the harder it'll get!" but he was grinning as he spoke, taking the edge off the truth of the statement.

Claire just shook her head and stumbled toward a tall oak that offered wide branches of shade, even though most of the leaves were on the ground, but all the better for a place to rest. Reuben turned to tend to his horse, stripping the gear off and stacking it near a pile of rocks, then grabbed a handful of oak leaves and used them to rub the horse down. He also loosened the harnesses on the mules but left them under gear, allowing them to go to graze nearby.

Eli had finished tending his mules and joined Claire and Martha at the oak tree with a bag of smoked meat and dried peaches which would be their lunch at this stop. Reuben soon finished and gathered some firewood to start a small cookfire. Eli glanced at Claire, "What's he doin'? Didn't think we was gonna have a reg'lar meal."

Claire chuckled, "He's gotta have his coffee. I haven't known him long but long enough to know he likes his coffee."

Martha added, "My pappy was like that, if we had it, he drank it. And when we didn't have it, he fussed about it!"

Reuben fashioned a tripod of saplings and hung the

coffee pot full of water over the fire and stood back to watch the flames lick the bottom of the pot. He grinned and sat down beside a big flat rock and started grinding some coffee beans for his brew. Within a few moments, he saw the pot beginning to dance and dropped in a big handful of grounds. He scraped the rest off the rock and put them in the bag with the beans to return to the wagon. With four cups in his hand, he returned to the fire to await the proper brewing of his nectar and soon smiled and started pouring steaming cups of coffee. With a broad smile, he walked to the others, holding out his offering and joined them as they watched over the children playing in the leaves.

"Plannin' on stayin' the night in Oskaloosa?" asked Eli, looking at Reuben over his cup.

"Nah, since we don't need any supplies, I thought we'd go right on through, maybe make the banks of the Des Moines river 'fore dark. Dependin' on the river and the light, maybe cross over and camp on the far side." He looked from one to the other, "Were you all thinkin' 'bout stoppin'?"

Claire answered, "No, but it would be nice if we talked about it before deciding."

Reuben dropped his head, grinned as he lifted his eyes to the others, "You're right. I'm sorry. I shouldn't have assumed anything without talkin' to you all. But, this leadin' folks is kinda new to me. I'm just used to takin' care of myself, was even like that in the army. Reckon that's why I fit so well with the sharpshooters, we'd all get orders, then go off on our own to carry 'em out."

"Well, you're not alone now and we're glad of it, too," replied Claire, smiling broadly as she reached out to lightly touch Reuben's arm.

"That's right, Reuben. We be mighty glad to be together with you folks. Just feels better, it do. Can't rightly explain it, but it do," responded Eli, glancing at Martha who was also smiling and nodding.

"I was meaning to ask you folks, what if others want to join us, you know, other wagons headin' west. I kinda thought we might run into other folks that might like to travel together. They say there's safety in numbers and what with all that's goin' on . . ." Reuben let the thought dangle for a moment, then added, "But could be we won't run into anybody else that's hankerin' to travel this time of year, what with winter comin' on and all."

Eli looked at his wife, back to Reuben, "It's be fine with us if'n we came acrost others what want to join us, cuz like you say, there's safety in numbers." Martha had scooted closer to her man and tucked her hand in at his elbow as she sat nodding her agreement.

"Isn't there also a risk in takin' folks along that we don't know?" asked Claire, frowning.

"Well, I reckon we can get to know them first, you know, have another one of your 'get acquainted' dinners," answered Reuben, grinning at Claire.

Claire grinned and bumped shoulders with Reuben who had sat down close to her. But Reuben, laughing, tried to keep his cup from spilling as he leaned away from her, "Whoa there girl, you 'most spilt my coffee!"

———

A TALL TIPPLE CAUGHT THEIR ATTENTION AS THEY NEARED the town. A narrow creek, whose bottom showed times of considerable flow, perhaps floodwaters, had been re-routed with a different channel that showed piles of hand shoveled dirt banks. But the presence of the mine shacks, the former creek bank dug out and a deep gouge that harbored a tunnel entrance with ore car tracks in the mouth, told of diggings, The growing pile of coal that stood near the tipple gave all the evidence needed of a prosperous coal mine. Several wagons were lined up beyond the tipple, waiting their turn for a load of coal, and a corral with mules, coats darkened by coal dust, showed the means of moving the ore carts. It was the end-of-shift and dirty-faced men were coming from the gaping maw of the tunnel, feet dragging and heads hanging. Reuben looked at the weary men, knew that many had been excused from the war as they were needed to mine the coal that would power the trains and wondered which was worse, the mine or the war.

They drew little attention as they drove their wagons down the main road through town. Even when they passed the town square that shouldered businesses all around, the busy folks who crowded the boardwalks were too attentive to their own errands and needs to pay any attention to 'movers' that were just passing through. Since the opening of the Oregon Trail and the western lands, the term had almost become synonymous with vagrant and worse. But now, during war times, many looked upon 'movers' as people that were running away from responsibility to do their part for the cause.

"Friendly town, isn't it?" commented Claire. Reuben had taken the lines of the mules, the horses were tethered behind, and Claire sat close beside him, Charlie at her other side.

"Ummhmm, maybe it's just the war. You notice there's a lot more women than men hereabouts," nodded Reuben.

"But still, the war affects everyone, so why not be civil and friendly?"

"They prob'ly are, with folks they know or that live nearby. But we're loaded up and passin' through. Don't pay to be friendly with folks you don't know, could be the enemy."

"Enemy? We're all Americans!" she declared.

Reuben shook his head, "But the way folks are now, that don't mean nuthin'. Some Americans are abolition-ists, some are southern sympathizers, some slavers, others not. Then there's the Copperheads and you don't know which way they think. So, it's not what someone looks like, it's what they believe and you can't see that. There are those that think if you don't believe like they do, you don't deserve to live, and they'd as sooner kill you as look at you!"

"It can't be that bad," frowned Claire, glancing from Reuben to the people on the boardwalks.

"Claire, that's the way it's always been. That's the way it was with the Revolutionary War. We were fighting people that looked just like us but believed different. Oh, I'm sure there have been wars when those that fought looked different and were easy to tell apart from those like yourself but not always. And the hard part is when it's your neighbor, schoolmate, fellow worker like those coal miners back there, and when they think different, they don't want to sit down and hash out the differences, they just want to wipe out those who believe different. That's what starts wars, Claire. That's what started this war. Don't you think I found it hard to pull the trigger on someone just cuz he had a different uniform? Don't you think I wondered what his name was? For all I knew, he could have been related but I had to pull the trigger and every time I did, someone died."

He slapped the leads to the mules to quicken their step and get them out of town and away from all the people, it wouldn't be soon enough. He sighed heavily, shook his head and looked sidelong at Claire, "I'm sorry, I didn't mean to start preaching."

"I understand, Reuben. It must have been hard for you."

"No harder for me than all the others, 'cept maybe the politicians that got us into this mess!"

The sun was dipping its colors below the western horizon as the two wagons neared the bank of the Des Moines River. A ferry was tied off to a massive elm tree that angled out over the water and the ferryman was standing beside a woman, his arm around her waist, as they enjoyed the colors of the sunset. Brilliant oranges faded to muted golds and dusty underbellies of the few low-hanging clouds. Long lances of gold shot high into the sky, piercing the high clouds, and splashing them with molten gold. The grey-haired man leaned his head atop that of his woman whose bonnet hid her silver locks. She was the first to turn toward the wagons and she nudged her man.

A broad smiling face, red-cheeked, with a bulbous red nose, looked at the new arrivals and he waved them close. "There's time 'nuff to get you acrost. Let's see," he leaned side to side to look at the wagons and animals, "travelin' together are ye?"

Reuben nodded, "That's right. One price for the bunch."

The old man grinned, "One dollar, six bits."

"Let's get 'em across then," answered Reuben.

The older man nodded, motioned to his wife who turned away to return to their cabin, and lowered the bar on the ferry, dragged out the loading planks and motioned the men to drive the wagons onto the ferry. It was a sizeable raft, wide enough for the wagons to side one another and the horses to be tethered behind. Everyone climbed down and stood at the rail as the ferry started across. It was a special sight to see the colors of the sunset bouncing off the ripples of the water and the splash of color that remained in the western sky. Before long, they bumped ashore and were once again on solid ground, much to the relief of Reuben and Eli. The men mounted the wagons after helping the women aboard and by the light of dusk, soon found a camp site for the night. Tomorrow would bring its own adventures.

"We," started Claire, nodding to Martha, "discovered that there's a backwater pool beyond the trees yonder and we decided we're going to bathe," she stated as she stood before Reuben and Eli. The men were starting to rig the teams but paused at the women's decision to delay their departure.

"And it wouldn't hurt for you two and the boys to do the same!" stated the usually quiet Martha, a slight grin lifting the corners of her mouth as a twinkle of mischief sparkled in her eyes. She glanced at Claire as they both stifled a giggle and turned away to fetch the necessities from the wagons.

Reuben looked at Eli, down at Charlie and Eli's two boys, "Huh, guess we been told!" and chuckled as he added, "Maybe we have been gettin' a little gamey!" as he sniffed his shirt.

"What's 'gamey'?" asked little Charlie, looking up at Reuben.

Reuben chuckled as he glanced at Eli, "Stink!" he answered.

Charlie nodded, "That's cuz we been travelin' an' playin' in the dirt!" he declared matter-of-factly.

"Well, we better fetch us some clean clothes or we'll hafta wash these. We can use a blanket or two to dry off with and keep us warm till we get dressed," said Reuben, his hand on Charlie's shoulder as he steered him to the wagon. Eli sent his boys to the wagon and he followed close after.

"It's all yours!" declared Claire as she returned to the campsite, running her fingers through her wet hair, a bundle of clothing over her arm. She wore a homespun grey linen dress trimmed with white lace at the collar and sleeves and her smile was radiant as she looked at Reuben. "That felt so good! Thank you for letting us have the time for that." She smiled coyly as she dropped her eyes, "And thanks for taking Charlie."

"He picked out his own clothes, so . . ." replied Reuben, glancing from Charlie to Claire. She was an attractive woman, and all woman, thought Reuben, giving her a lingering look. "Be sure to keep your Paterson handy and your shotgun within reach. We'll be back shortly."

Charlie tugged at his sleeve, "C'mon Reuben, let's go!" he demanded.

Reuben smiled down at the anxious youngster and motioned, "Lead the way, Charlie. But don't go in till I do!" He watched as the boy took off at a run, trying to catch up to Amos and Andrew as they walked beside Eli. He had his Remington Army revolver in the holster at his hip, but he picked up the Henry to take with, just to be on the safe side.

After a spell of splashing and sudsing, the five soon climbed the grassy bank to dry off and put on the fresh clothes. They had followed the directions of the women and took the dirty clothes in the water with them and scrubbed and rinsed everything including the holey long underwear that now hung on the willows catching the cool breeze. As they dressed, Charlie looked at the boys and their dad and asked, "How come God painted you dark?"

Eli chuckled and spoke in his deep bass voice, "Same reason God painted you light!"

"I never saw darkies afore but you're just like us, 'ceptin' the color," added Charlie, his innocence showing as he struggled with his brogans.

"Well, did you ever think that people are just like everything else God made, a little different on the outside, but just the same on the inside?" drawled Eli.

"Really?" asked Charlie.

"Sure 'nuff. Come along and let me show you sumpin'," said Eli, motioning his boys and Charlie to follow. He nodded to Reuben and started into the woods. He spotted a big poplar tree and walked to it, took out his knife and pointed to the almost black bark, "Now see here, the outside of this tree is real dark," he held his arm up close, "kinda like my skin. But lookee here." He cut away a piece of the bark exposing the inner bark of the tree, "See this?" he pointed to the pale inner bark and wood, "I'm gonna cut a piece of this and we'll take it with us." He sliced off a piece about three inches by two and handed it to Charlie.

Eli spotted a small grove of birch and walked close, reached out to the white bark and said, "Now this bark is white, kinda like you, Charlie. But watch this." He peeled off a piece of the bark and exposed the soft wood, "See here, it's just like that piece you have in your hand." He sliced off a similarly-sized piece and handed it to Amos.

They repeated the action when they encountered a

silver maple and Eli gave the slice of wood to Andrew. Eli grinned, "Now, pass the pieces to each other, go on," he began, "And again," and watched as the boys passed the pieces several times. When they looked up again, Eli said, "Now, which piece came from the black barked poplar?"

The boys looked from one to the other, and back again, confused expressions on their faces.

Eli added, "And which one came from the white barked birch?" he paused and watched their expressions. With a broad smile, he added, "Remember, they were all different on the outside but much the same on the inside. So, don't forget this lesson as you meet other people. They might be different than you on the outside, but . . ." and he shrugged his shoulders as he motioned the boys back to camp.

As they neared the wagons, the boys ran ahead, eager to share their newfound knowledge with their mothers but they drew up short when they saw a strange man, sitting his horse and leaning on the pommel of his saddle speaking to the women and Reuben. When the boys skidded to a stop beside their mothers, Reuben grinned at the youngsters and looked back at the man on the horse. He was a lanky man, looked to be in his mid-twenties, with a black frock coat, vest, linen striped britches, and black boots. The butt of a pistol showed between his vest and coat, the bulge evident at his waist. His thin face was topped with a flat-brimmed black hat with a thin silver band. Deep-set dark eyes rode high cheekbones and wavy black hair hung to his collar.

"So, you a gambler?" asked Reuben.

The man grinned, tipped his hat back and chuckled, looking down at his attire and answered, "You could say that, prob'ly thought that because I'm wearing black. But no, I'm not what most folks would call a gambler." He shifted his weight, leaned forward, "I'm Parson Page. I'm bound for Fort Kearny and thought I might ride along with you folks, if that's alright?"

"Why you goin' to Fort Kearny?" asked Reuben.

"Goin' to start a church. Seems there's a lot of new settlers in the area and my church leaders received a letter asking for a parson. So, I was anxious to go west and here I am."

"I thought all pastors were married?" asked Claire, frowning.

"Most are, after a spell. But I recently graduated seminary at William Jewell College and haven't really been where there were a lot of young ladies. But my professor thought I should also consider becoming a missionary to the plains Indians and that wouldn't be too safe for a lady."

Reuben glanced at Eli as he joined the group, turned to ask him, "This parson fella would like to ride along with us. He's also going to Fort Kearny, any objections?"

"Why no, I don't have no objections. Might be nice to have a parson along, maybe have Sunday services."

Reuben shook his head, turned back to the Parson, "I never saw a pistol packin' parson before. You know how to use that?" nodding to the bulge at his waist.

"I do. Carry it for snakes, you know, both those that crawl and those that walk. Can't be too careful in this country in these times."

"Might be good to have an extra man, so, it's all right with us if you join. You'll hafta carry your own weight and that means occasionally driving a wagon, getting game, and so on. Might get your hands dirty."

"That's fine, mighty fine." He looked at the first wagon, saw the mules and stepped down to help with the harness. Within moments, he proved he knew his way around the mules and gear and was eager to prove his worth. Reuben grinned, thought of his mother, and knew she would be pleased and if still alive, she would be tickled, that he would be traveling with someone that, in her way of thinking, knew the Word and wouldn't hesitate to share it.

Reuben chose to lead off by scouting far ahead. Parson Page had volunteered to handle the mules for Claire and joined her on the spring seat. He was no stranger to handling a team of mules and Reuben thought that in his youth he must have been on a farm and handled a team, probably behind a plow. He was not sure what to think of the Parson but he would bide his time and keep a wary eye. Just because he dressed and talked like one, did not necessarily mean he really was a parson, but if he was, the rest of the folks liked the idea of having a man of the cloth along.

"They're callin' themselves the Home Guard but some of 'em are organizing as the Southern Border Brigade. But whatever they's callin' themselves, we gotta be armed and ready for 'em." It was a small cavalcade of rag-tag, wannabe soldiers, the only uniform being home-spun, embroidered shirts with garish but colorful designs. The leader was Fletch Taylor, a lieutenant of Captain William Quantrill, recently commissioned a captain under the Confederate Partisan Ranger Act of 1862. "The Home Guard has made a few excursions into our territory and now it's our turn. The Captain said we need supplies and we're to get 'em any way we see fit! George Todd and his bunch are hittin' 'em further west near the Kansas border and we'll take any farms and such straight north of here."

"We gonna hit any towns, Fletch?" asked his right-hand man, Beauregard, 'Bob', Bridger. Bob was a big man, full beard and scraggly hair, his shirt was a pattern of blue flowers and bright sun, neither seemed appropriate for the foul-mouthed brigand. His rump seemed to hang over both sides of his scrawny horse and most wondered how the horse could carry such a load. His gravelly voice grated and was sometimes hard to understand.

"We might, but first we're gonna keep outa sight, scoutin' targets as we go north, then we'll hit 'em on the way back south. That way we can keep on the run 'fore any o' the Home Guard can come after us."

'Booger' Blunt rode behind Fletch and, having heard the tactics of their leader, said, "We gotta be careful we don't wind the horses. That's all we need is to be on the run with wore out nags under us."

"Maybe we can get us some new ones on one o' them farms," suggested 'Pickles' Baxter, the smallest of the bunch but also known as the bloodiest. Whenever they got in a fight, Pickles always managed to be the one nearest any women and would be almighty quick with his Bowie knife that he kept razor sharp. Whenever the fight was over, he was usually bloodied head to foot and the others would often throw him into any nearby creek to clean him up and stay the stink.

"Want me a mule!" grumbled 'Bull' Anderson. He was bigger than any of the others, including Bob Bridger but, where Bob was fat, Bull's name was descriptive for he was built like a bull. Broad shouldered, barrel chested and mounted on legs that resembled tree trunks, he earned his name when he wrestled a big bull to the ground and twisted the bull's neck until it was dead. "Mules are smarter'n horses and a good 'un won't have any trouble carryin' me!" he proclaimed to no one in particular. He glanced to the side at their newest member, "Whattaboutchu Woody, you wantin' 'nother ride?"

"Muh name's not Woody!" growled the youngster. He had joined the bunch when they passed through his home country in Clay County, Missouri. He was tired of his mother's new husbands, she was now on her third one and they were poppin' out kids faster than the farm stock. "Just cuz my middle name is Woodson, I ain't Woody! My name's Jesse!" he whined. The boy was so thin he would have to stand in the same place twice to cast a shadow. He was tall and lanky, dark hair in widow peaks, but his eyes were steely and dark, the kind that held secrets and were always plotting, usually for something evil. He never said how old he was but the others guessed him to be about fifteen. When he wasn't near, the others just referred to him as 'the kid,' but when they found out the kid was quick with his pistol and deadlier than a den of rattlesnakes, they were respectful of his wants.

"So, you want a new ride, Jesse?" corrected Bull, grumbling and snarling at the youth.

"If I can find a good one, one that'll stretch out and run but still have good wind. I kinda favor the strawberry roan but they're hard to find." Bull nodded as he looked around at the thick trees and underbrush. Although most of the trees were naked of leaves, the brush still tried to reach up and snag at the britches and blankets of the passersby.

Fletch was twisting his way through the thickets when he held up his hand to stop the group. He leaned over his pommel, looking at a field that sided a farm house and barns, "That looks like a good place. See there, they've got horses in that corral by the barn."

"That's not too far from the other'n we spotted this mornin'," replied Bob.

"Ummhmmm. That makes three good targets. We'll keep movin' till we find at least three more. And dependin' on time, we'll turn in for the night and start in the mornin' to make our way back." He paused a moment, still looking over the farm, "Captain Quantrill said the further we go into their territory, the more effective the attack. He said it discourages and frightens them abolitionists, makes 'em vulnerable."

"If we wait till mornin', Todd and his bunch might hit first and the Guard will head thataway," surmised Bob.

"Exactly. And Todd thinks he's somethin' special so if he gets hit hard by the Guard, maybe he won't be so high and mighty!" replied Fletch. It was no secret that Fletch and Todd had been bitter rivals since the onset of the war. Todd had been trying for his own commission but had been passed over in favor of Quantrill and, for some reason, thought Fletch Taylor was to blame.

The Bushwhackers continued on their foray, careful to keep their presence quiet until they were ready to start their strike. They had followed the Waldon River north out of Missouri, and it was now little more than a small creek. There had been signs near the roads of different settlements, Garden Grove, Corydon, Richmond, Bartlettville, Chariton, and others, but they kept to the low swales, the thick forests, anything to mask their presence.

Quantrill wanted them to get close to Osceola, so the strike would make everyone remember when the pro-union Red Legs under U.S. senator James H. Lane, made an assault on Osceola, Missouri, executed nine men and plundered and burned the town to the ground, leaving behind the dead for the buzzards and carrion eaters. The cry, "Remember Osceola," would be heard many times before the war was over.

It was two days since they left Missouri and the sun was lowering in the west to mark an end of their foray north. Now was the time to find a good hidden camp, get some rest and make ready for their southern assault.

———

"WILLIAM JEWELL COLLEGE, AIN'T THAT DOWN IN Missouri?" asked Reuben. They were sitting around the cookfire enjoying the after-dinner coffee and the cool of the evening. The stars were lighting their lanterns, the nightbirds were tuning up for their serenade of darkness, and the travelers were basking in the warmth of the fire.

The Parson lifted his eyes from the flames, looked at the shadowy figure of Reuben and answered, "It is in Liberty, Missouri, this side of Independence."

"Wasn't there a battle of some sort, early on, down there?"

"There was. Some have called it the Battle of Liberty. Happened while I was at school and they turned the college into a field hospital and buried their dead on the campus. Gave all the college kids and staff an up close look at what war was really like." He shook his head at the memory. "Also gave several of us an opportunity to minister to the dying, helped to bring them to Christ before they died." He paused, staring at the fire, and continued, "It's always amazing how even the biggest and bravest are fearful when they know they're about to meet their maker. But even *they* are eager to know the truth of what their mothers had tried to tell them, or what they knew as children and maybe had wandered away, and to be given the opportunity to make things right, was and always is comforting."

Reuben squirmed a little on the rough-barked log, picked up a chunk of firewood and lay it on the fire, and looked at the parson, "But what about those that had killed men? Even in the thick of a battle when they're fighting for their lives, they still pulled the trigger and sent another man to his grave. That weighs heavy on a man's heart, even though as a child he knew the Lord as his Savior, killing goes against the commandment. Doesn't it say, *Thou shalt not kill?*"

"Yes, Reuben, God gave his commandments to Moses and the sixth commandment is *Thou shalt not kill.* But, throughout the Bible there are many examples of having to kill to protect others; you remember the story of David and Goliath and David said, *'I come to thee in the name of the Lord,'* and he slew, or killed, the giant to save his people. And there are many other times that death was dealt to save the lives of others. So, what I believe the commandment means is *Thou shalt not commit murder.* And when you or anyone lifts their hand to save another and has to deal out death, that is not against His Law."

"So, if someone like me that has killed so many in war and others as well, even though I accepted Christ as my savior when I was younger, God can forgive me?"

"That's right, I believe that with my whole heart," nodded Parson Page, glancing from Reuben to the others. "And there will probably times when both of us," pointing to Reuben and to himself, "will have to defend those we care about and maybe take the life of another, perhaps some raiders or Indians or highwaymen, and others will die at our hand but sometimes that will happen and we have no choice and God totally understands."

Reuben sighed heavily, shrugged, and said, "That's good to know. I was beginning to have doubts about that whole salvation thing, you know, being saved like my Momma always talked about."

Parson Page nodded, "I understand and, if you ever want to talk more about it, I'm here to listen and help."

Reuben nodded, rose, "I think I'll check on the animals," and faded into the darkness.

Parson Page had traveled with them for two days but was already readily accepted as one of them. He was a hard worker, eager to help and please, but always firm in his beliefs. He had been driving the wagon for Claire but would be riding with Reuben tomorrow, scouting ahead on the crude roadway made by the railroad workers in preparation of laying track. Reuben thought they would reach Osceola late tomorrow and, if necessary, resupply before pushing on to the Missouri River and into Nebraska territory. Parson thought about their journey and knew that once they crossed the Missouri, they would be in Indian territory and their challenges would increase, but all travel could be hazardous, especially in these times.

"So, you said you knew about that 'salvation' thing from when you were a boy. Tell me about it," suggested Parson Page. He and Reuben were riding well out front of the wagons, scouting the trail and territory for the slow-moving wagons and their precious cargo of women and children. The last sign of any settlement was a crudely lettered sign that pointed to the little berg of Newbern, about a mile off the roadway. But that was just after sunup and they had been on the trail for most of the morning. Reuben was normally a quiet man but Pastor Page had made it his business to learn more about those in his meager and nomadic congregation.

"Well, my Momma used to keep the family in church, back in White Pigeon. We kinda grew up in church. So the preacher would lay out the Scripture, you know, where it says *Except a man be born again, he cannot see the kingdom of God,'* and tell about how Jesus died for our sins and gives a free gift of eternal life if we but trust Him. And he'd talk about how to trust Him, we had to believe in our heart and call on Him in prayer, ask Him to forgive our sins and come into our heart and save us.

So, when the preacher gave his invitation for all us sinners to come up and kneel and pray what he called the 'Sinner's Prayer,' that's just what I did. I went up, knelt down, and prayed for all I was worth so He would save my soul and I believe He did just that. Made me feel awful good after that."

He paused as he looked to the trees, remembering his youth, "And it wasn't till I went off to war, became a sharpshooter, when I had to hunt down them Confederates and shoot 'em, that I began to wonder 'bout things."

Parson glanced at Reuben, looked to the trail ahead as he waited, then saw movement at the edge of the trees. He frowned, leaned to the side for a better look, and glanced to Reuben, "What's that over there by that fence?"

His tone was quiet but concerned, immediately rousing Reuben's attention. He looked ahead to where the Parson motioned, then nudged the sorrel to a trot, watching the fence and all the trees and brush nearby. The men reined up and stepped down, Reuben had his Henry in hand and was looking around for any sign of others. The figure leaned against the bottom rail of the fence and the Parson went to his side. The man was bloodied, looked like he had been dragged and probably shot once or twice, but he was alive. Through the trees, Reuben saw smoke and smelled the awful stench of burning flesh. He glanced to the unconscious man, "He gonna live?" he asked the Parson.

"Dunno. He's hurt bad. Been shot once in the shoulder, another'n in the leg, but he was dragged and that tore him up somethin' fierce." The Parson rose and went to his saddlebags for something to cleanse and bandage the man.

Reuben asked, "Can you handle him? I'm gonna

check out the farm, see if the ones what done it are still around."

"Go ahead. I can handle this and the wagons'll be along soon."

"If I ain't back 'fore they get here, keep 'em away, and keep your weapon handy. You got a rifle?"

"In the scabbard."

Reuben went to the Parson's scabbard that hung beneath the right stirrup fender and withdrew the rifle. He frowned as he looked at the weapon, glanced to the Parson and shook his head, "This is one o' them Spencers ain't it?"

"That's right. Right fine rifle that."

"Keep it handy," added Reuben as he started through the trees.

———

Fletch Taylor stood behind the thick trunk of a big oak, watching an older farmer come from the barn carrying a milk bucket that sloshed white over the edge. A thin spiral of smoke from the chimney of the house showed the stillness of the morning. Nothing else moved, all the animals were either in the barn or in the field, and no other workers, if there were any, had shown themselves. Fletch turned back to his men, sitting on their horses, waiting his signal, and spoke softly. "We'll ride up real slow like, looking peaceable. If the old man comes out, we'll see if his woman wants to fix breakfast for us and, if there ain't no others, we'll hit fast and hard." He looked from one to the other, and with his focus on Pickles, added, "Wait for me to make the first move," he growled as he mounted his big black.

Fletch pushed through the brush and cleared the

trees, took to the roadway that led to the clearing in front of the house, and reined up at the side door where he had seen the farmer enter. He called out, "Hello the house! Anybody about?" He sat quietly on his saddle, doing his best to look friendly and non-threatening. "We're from the Home Guard, passin' through!" he hollered a little louder. He waited until the door opened and the farmer stood looking out over the barrel of a shotgun. "Whoa, there's no need for that. We're with the Home Guard, thought you might have some biscuits to spare. We're on the move to the border and ain't got time for breakfast. We got orders that some o' Quantrill's guerillas are tryin' to cross into Iowa after the abolitionists and we're s'posed to stop 'em. But we don't wanna put you out none."

He acted like he was going to rein his mount around to leave but the farmer called out, "Now hold on! Lemme see if Ma's got some biscuits to spare." He lowered the shotgun and started to turn back to the inside and Fletch snatched his pistol from his shoulder holster and blasted away, dropping the man before he could turn around.

The shot opened the ball and the others cut loose, riddling the windows and door of the farm house with bullets, the barrage sounding like rolling thunder. The Bushwhackers started yelling and screaming like crazed banshees. Bob Bridger motioned for Booger Blunt and Jesse to follow him and they headed for the barn. Pickles and Bull stayed with Fletch and after another round of bullets into the windows, the two slid to the ground and started into the farmhouse, Fletch staying outside to oversee the plundering and destruction. He nudged his mount toward the barn, heard some shooting and screaming and slapped legs to the horse. He charged into the dark interior, saw Bridger and

James at the edge of the stalls, firing toward the back door.

Fletch swung down, hollered at Bridger, "How many?"

"Just one, but he ain't shot back. I think he run off!"

"I'll go around," replied Fletch, climbing back aboard his mount. He jerked the horse's head around, dug heels into his ribs and lunged from the barn. He lay low as he rounded the corner of the barn, charging to the back. He snatched at his riata, loosened the loop, and turned the corner of the barn at a run. He saw a man stumbling into the field and he gave chase. He swung the loop over his head and within a few bounds had overtaken the man and dropped the loop over his head and shoulders. The man stumbled as Fletch jerked slack but Fletch didn't let up and kept the horse running, jerking the man from his feet and dragging him through the corn stubble. After about fifty yards, he reined up, moved back toward the crumpled and bloody form that was a man and stepped down to remove his riata. As he turned away, the man groaned and Fletch snatched his pistol, turned and fired into the body, laughing and snarling, "That'll teach you to be one o' them abolitionists!" He holstered his pistol, coiled his riata, and climbed aboard to return to the others.

When Pickles and Bull stormed into the house, they stepped over the bullet-riddled body of the old man, saw the woman sitting on the floor, her back against the stove and head hanging down. She had taken at least three bullets, one in the neck and two in her chest. Pickles cackled as he brought out his knife, feeling its sharpness with his thumb and glaring at the woman. Bull said, "Check the back rooms!"

"Sure, Bull, I can do that!" he cackled as he started to

the door off the kitchen. He pushed it open to the sound of a scream and lunged into the room, knife extended, and slammed the door behind him. Bull shook his head and went to the stove, pushed the smoking frying pan off the hot spot, and picked up the bacon, grinning as he smacked his lips. He downed the entire pan full, glanced at the table where a plate of biscuits sat and continued his feast with the biscuits. He heard the ruckus from the closed room, shook his head knowingly and chose not to interfere with Pickle's party. He cleaned the plate of all the biscuits, glanced around and saw the coffee pot still on the stove, grabbed a cup from the table and poured some steaming coffee into the tin cup, and started drinking, unmindful of the hot liquid.

The door slammed open and a bloodied Pickles stood grinning and laughing hysterically, looked from Bull to the door, saw the doorway to the main room and started rummaging for anything of value. While Bull finished the coffee and the rest of a cake he found in the cupboard, Pickles discovered a stash of bills and coins in a tin on the shelf with some books. He threw the books on the floor and began to pile chairs and little tables in the middle of the floor. He grabbed a lamp, pulled a Lucifer from his pocket, and struck it to light the lamp, threw the oil lamp atop the pile of chairs and cackled as it burst and flame covered the pile, fingers of fire reaching for the ceiling.

"Let's go Bull! It's a burnin'!" shouted Pickles as he ran for the open door but as he started out, he saw the body of the man was gone. He frowned, looking about, but quickly stepped outside, his eyes on a blood trail. He followed what appeared to be drag marks and realized the farmer was dragging himself around the back of the house. Pickles spotted him crawling into the garden area and he walked up behind, cackling as he felt the tip of his knife. The farmer whimpered as Pickles straddled him, grabbed his hair, and jerked his head back. While the farmer tried to struggle free, Pickles put his knife at the farmer's forehead and sliced off his scalp, dropped the man's head and walked away, scalp in hand, cackling like a lunatic. Bull grunted, glanced at the growing fire, and quickly exited the house, satisfied after his feast. He started for the root cellar and threw open the slanted door, dropping into the dark interior. He grabbed a toe sack and began filling it with dried vegetables and fruits, filled another with potatoes, slung the two bags over his shoulder and picked up a crock of pickled meat and started for the horses.

Booger and Jesse led two horses from the barn while Bob was struggling with a recalcitrant mule. He leaned back against the lead rope just as the mule sat back on his hind legs, glaring at the man that was demanding that he follow. Bob stood up, loosening the lead, talked to the mule, "C'mon you stubborn worthless hunk o' hairy hide!" and leaned against the line again. Making no progress, he turned, put the lead over his shoulder and tried pulling against the lop-eared mule but again no progress.

Booger handed off the lead to the horse to Jesse, turned back to where Bob was struggling with the mule, walked past Bob and pulled the pistol from his belt and shot the mule behind his ear. The beast dropped instantly, Bob fell on his face and came up cussing. Booger just shook his head and walked back to Jesse and started rigging the packsaddle on the bay gelding, readying it for the load that Bull was carrying toward them.

Fletch returned, saw the dead mule, and watched as

Bob put a torch to the barn. He grinned as he saw the bounty taken from the root cellar, saw Bull nod toward Pickles and knew the mousy Pickles had found something more. He nudged his mount toward the bloody lunatic. "Hand it over," said Fletch, holding his hand out, palm up and waiting.

Pickles mumbled as he dug into his shirt, reaching for a draw-string pouch had found in the house with the money, and handed it up to Fletch. He wouldn't look at Fletch, guilt turning his gaze aside as he whined, "How'd you know?"

"I always know, Pickles. And don't forget it!"

As Reuben neared the edge of the trees, he dropped to one knee, searching the farm yard for any movement. His eyes moved across the yard, saw the usual well house, the root cellar with the door flipped back revealing the steps to the dark interior. He scanned past the rail fence that joined the barn, saw nothing in the corral, nor in the trees that stood nearby. The remains of the house smoldered, grey and black smoke lazily spiraling upwards, while the larger barn still blazed, and as he watched, the roof crashed inward, sending a shower of embers and smoke rising in a bulbous cloud. With every image, his mind flashed with the memories of his own family farm, his family in the graves, and the other farms burnt and pillaged by the phony Home Guard bunch. He shook his head, clearing his mind, looked to the field to see a milk cow running from the conflagration, her bag bouncing between her legs and a calf bounding along after. Overhead, turkey buzzards were already circling, watching the farmyard for possible pickings.

After another thorough scan, Reuben breathed heavily. He was satisfied there was no one nearby. He slowly stepped from the trees; his Henry rifle held across his chest as he walked toward the rubble that had once been the farmhouse. He glanced to a torn-down fence to the side of the house, saw where a garden spot had been trampled and plundered. What he thought had been a scarecrow proved to be the mutilated body of a farmer, grey head showing blood where he had been scalped. His body lay stretched out where he had tried to crawl away, but now two crows were determined to get the better of a young eagle as they picked at his neck and cheek.

He looked to the barn, saw the carcass of a mule sprawled near the door and saw the turkey buzzards start to descend, focused on the mule. The smell of burning flesh wafted over him as he walked closer to front of the house. He lifted his neckerchief to cover his mouth and nose and stepped into the blackened remains. The kitchen stove stood under burnt timbers and Reuben saw a woman's shoe. He knew the rest of her body was under the timbers and ashes. He pulled away two burnt pieces and the body fell forward, her back where the apron strings were tied in a bow, untouched as she rested against the front of the stove.

Stepping over her body, he picked his way toward the back wall, a burnt partition separating a back room from the front room with the fireplace. The remains of a four-poster bed, handmade, partially sheltered the body of a young woman recognizable only by one hand and shoulder that lay under the bed. A tiny ring with a small blue stone was on the ring finger.

He stepped over the half wall that remained at the back of the house and started for the barn but stopped, knowing if anything were in there it would be burnt to ashes. Reuben dropped his eyes, walked to the root cellar, and bent to look in, saw empty shelves, broken jugs and urns on the floor, and big boot tracks on the dusty steps. He stood, took another look around, and started back to the trees.

The wagons were stopped in the roadway; the victim of the attack had been stretched out on a blanket atop the grassy edge and Claire and Martha were busy tending to the man. Reuben saw Parson and Eli standing back and watching, and he walked to them. As he neared, both men looked up, nodded, and waited for him to tell what he found. But Reuben asked, "Has he said anything?"

"Just asked about his family. Said somethin' about Bushwhackers and Quantrill but couldn't quite make it out," answered the Parson. "What'd you find?"

"His family," answered Reuben, dropping his head. He glanced up to Eli, "We're gonna need some shovels and maybe pull the wagons aside. Parson, how 'bout you stayin' here with the women folk, just in case, while me'n Eli take care of the dead?"

"If it's all the same to you, I'd rather help you, maybe say a few words for the family," suggested the Parson.

Reuben glanced from Eli to the Parson, nodded and reached for the reins of the sorrel and stopping by the wagon pulled out a couple blankets and started back through the brush. He was quiet as he neared what was left of the farmhouse, turned to the Parson, "Mayhap you could look around, perhaps by the trees and such, see if you can find a family plot to bury these folks," and nodded toward the back of the house.

It was a gruesome but familiar task that Reuben undertook as he started sorting through the blackened timbers and ashes to gather the remains of the women. He put them together on one blanket and covered them over before going to the body of the man with the second blanket. In short order, he had rigged a bit of a sled for the remains to pull behind the horse to where the Parson had been digging the graves. Once the bodies were interred, the Parson stood at the head of the three graves and committed the dead to the hands of his God.

Before they started back, they stopped at the well and washed up, a bar of lye soap and a ragged towel sat on the edge of the well and they put it to good use. As they walked back to the wagons, the Parson looked at Reuben, "I somehow get the feeling you are planning something, am I right?"

"Ummhmmm, and I'd like to know the rest," nodding toward the wagons and the others, "will be in good hands while I'm gone."

"Gone? Are you planning on going after those that did this dastardly thing?" asked the Parson, somewhat incredulous.

"If I'm right, these men will keep doing this until they're stopped. And like my Pa used to say, *when evil raises its ugly head, good men have to make things right. And if you see yourself as a good man, then it's up to you.* Men just like these killed my family, burnt my farm, and if I had not chased them down and stopped their evil, they would still be killing and burning just like this bunch. Look around, Parson. You see anybody else doing anything to stop them?"

"Why no, but . . ."

"Parson, you can preach all you want against evil but, if all we do is talk about it, then evil will never be stopped. Now, the way I see it, my being here was no accident, so . . ." and Reuben looked away as they neared the wagons. The injured man was sitting up against the big wagon wheel and Reuben went to one knee beside him. "What can you tell me about those that hit your place?"

The man frowned, "When they first came to the farm, I was in the loft an' I heard 'em tell Pa they were from the Home Guard, so I went about my feeding. But I heard two of 'em talking when they came into the barn," he struggled as he spoke, his pain showing in his eyes but he continued. "I heard them say 'Captain Quantrill wants any horses and supplies we find. This is the first place and there's only two horses, he ain't gonna be none too happy,' and then I tried to sneak out the back but they saw me, shot me in the leg, and when I ran, another one roped and dragged me through the cornfield, then he shot me and laughed. I heard him say something about teachin' me to be an abolitionist."

He struggled to shift positions, fought for breath, and asked, "My family?"

"We found an older man and woman and a young woman, dead."

The man choked off a sob, "My folks and sister."

"We didn't have names for a marker but maybe you can tell the Parson and he and Eli can make something suitable," offered Reuben, glancing back to Eli. He stood, went to the back of the wagon, and started gathering what he would need for his jaunt. Claire came to his side, "You going after them?"

"Got to," he answered, glancing at her. "You understand."

"Yes, but I'm afraid for you."

"The Parson and Eli will still be with you and you'll be safe. Hopefully, this won't take long and I'll catch up soon."

"Please do, and be careful," she said as she touched his arm.

When he finished packing his bedroll, a few extras, and stuffed the saddlebags with rations and ammunition, he strapped everything on the saddle, including his Sharps in a scabbard on the left side and the Henry in a scabbard on the right. He turned to Eli and the Parson and bent to the ground to draw a crude map. "We're here, just east of Osceola. Now from here, head due west until you get to the Missouri. Cross it, prob'ly find a ferry, and continue due west till you come to the Blue River. Cross it, then follow the north fork to the headwaters, keep west till you hit the Platte, and follow it till you come to Fort Kearny."

"Looks easy 'nuff," declared Eli, nodding.

"Looks can be deceiving," added the Parson.

"Well, I hope to catch up to you long before you get to the Missouri, but . . ." and he left the thought hanging as he stood and turned to mount the sorrel. He looked down at the small group, tipped his hat, and nudged the sorrel into the trees to take the trail after the Bushwhackers.

Within a couple miles, Reuben, staying on the trail of the raiders, crossed a main road with signs showing Osceola to the west and Glenn to the east and, within another mile, he came to White Breast Creek, a little further he crossed the south fork of the White Breast Creek. The tracks of the raiders varied little in their direction, always bearing due south. Reuben thought, *They have their route planned out, never changing direction, always bound for their next farm. What is it about men like this that have no regard for human life and the way of others? This isn't war, it's mayhem, murder!* He reckoned there were always those of such a selfish and immoral bent that, no matter who or where, they were bound to take what they wanted regardless of the price that others had to pay. He shook his head, disgusted, as he put leg pressure to the sorrel to quicken his pace.

The raiders were keeping away from roads, choosing dim trails in the woods or keeping to the swales and dips of the land, avoiding detection from any troops or lawmen that might be in the area but Reuben was bound to their trail by his resolve to end their reign of pillaging and plunder. It was just past mid-day when he smelled smoke and reined up, searching the treetops and hills for any sign of smoke but nothing showed against the clear blue fall sky. A cool breeze bathed his face as he looked to the southwest and, with a fresh whiff of burning flesh, he gigged his horse in that direction.

Crossing the trail of the raiders, he knew he was moving toward another burnt farm and probably the remains of the family that made it their home. A low rise lifted him above the scene where all that stood was a lone stone chimney and blackened ground. Whatever had been there was completely obliterated by the raging conflagration. Thin wisps of smoke lifted like ghostly fingers rising from the dead but their only message was of death.

Reuben rode near enough to see the raiders had already fled the scene, and he saw no need to see more. Even from where he sat, he could see the bodies of two milk cows in the corral, the body of a man near the barn, and smell the stench of burning flesh and see the ashes of dreams. He dug heels to his horse, taking after the trail of the raiders. He had some time to make up but, with their continual stopping to kill and plunder, he might catch them before dark, hopefully.

After crossing the Chariton River, Reuben came to a crossing roadway with a sign showing Bartlettville to the east and Garden Grove about five miles to the south, probably on the route of the raiders. He passed two poor farms with dugouts for homes, lean-tos for any animals, and none realized how fortunate they were to have so little, for the raiders were hitting only the established and apparently prosperous farms with more bounty and horses that were needed by Quantrill.

It was a thickly forested area he was passing through

and had it been earlier in the season, the trail would be difficult to follow but, now, with the trees standing like naked banshees, the wind whistling through the barren branches, the trail of the raiders was evident where their horses had trampled the wet leaves in their rush to the next target. He soon broke from the trees and found himself atop a slight knoll giving him a good view of the lowlands and farms. He twisted in his saddle and picked the binoculars from his saddlebags. They had been standard issue for the sharpshooters assigned to singular patrols and targets but, now, served a better purpose. His horse stood with head raised and ears pricked as in the distance the sound of gunfire was rattling across the flats. It rolled across the farmlands like a gathering thunderstorm and Reuben hoped it might warn someone but feared the farmers, always intent on the weather, would be hopeful of a late rainstorm. He searched the terrain for smoke but it was a short while before he saw the first pillar of grey rise from the now barren farm fields. Harvests had been gathered, bounty laid up in lofts and sheds, and the fields had only dry stubble as reminders of what once was a proud crop of corn, wheat, oats, or potatoes.

The smoke rose from a low-lying swale just beyond some rolling hills and even with binoculars, Reuben could not see the targeted farm. Quickly replacing the field glasses, he slapped legs to the sorrel and leaned forward to encourage the weary animal. They took a direct route to the smoke, bypassing the trail of the raiders, hopeful of gaining ground, maybe even catching them amid their raids. But when he sighted the farm, he knew he was late, three buildings blazed like matching cookfires and again the smell of burning flesh greeted an angry Reuben. He rode quickly among the fires, looking for any obvious survivors, passed the family burial plot and noted the names on the gravestones but, seeing no sign of survivors, reined the sorrel away to take to the trail of the raiders once again. He knew he would have to stop soon before the sorrel gave out on him and a quick thought spurred him on toward the nearby settlement of Garden Grove.

The trail of the raiders kept them on the west side of the Weldon River but when Reuben came to a crossroad and saw a sign that pointed east showing Garden Grove, one mile, he turned toward town. It wasn't much of a town, the main road showed three buildings on one side, two on the other, and a livery at the end. On one side of the road sat a tavern, an emporium, and a sheriff's office. The other side had a tavern and smaller building with a sign that said *Ma's Eats*. Reuben grinned and walked the sorrel to the livery, stepped down as he was greeted at the door by a whiskered face, "Howdy stranger! What kin I do ye fer?" He spoke with a voice that sounded like a squeaky and rusty barn door. It grated on Reuben but he forced himself not to wince at the verbal assault.

"Well, if you're the liveryman, I need some grain for my horse, a good rubdown, and a mite of water and hay. Won't be long, I'm headin' to Ma's for a meal."

"I kin get the grain fer your nag but I ain't givin' you no rubdown!" he cackled as he spat a gob of tobacco, the juice trailing through his whiskers on a familiar path.

"Not me! The horse!" laughed Reuben.

"Oh, wal, that's differ'nt. I kin do all that fer, uh, four bits!"

Reuben flipped him two coins, laughing, and watched as the man dropped his chair to all four legs, snapped his braces, and started to the sorrel. Reuben started to the café, anxious for a good meal. When he stepped through the door, he was assaulted by the aroma of biscuits and more, making him pause and breathe in the wonderful smells, such a dramatic change from what he had passed at the last farm. He grinned as he took a seat at a table by the big window, noticed two older men sitting at one of the other tables, and looked up as a portly woman with a bright yellow apron and a broad smile came his way. "Howdy stranger! Hungry are ya?"

"Yes ma'am. And I'll have whatever you're cooking that smells so good!" declared Reuben, leaning back in the chair to look up at the woman.

She smiled even more, her eyes dancing with mischief, "That's what I like! A hungry man that ain't partic'lar." She turned toward the other men with one eyebrow raised in reproach as she turned back to the kitchen. The last of her words an obvious condemnation of the men she glared at as she passed.

She soon returned with a big platter holding a thick steak, potatoes with gravy, two biscuits and green beans. In her other hand was a steaming cup of coffee. She sat the fixings down before Reuben and looked at him with an expression that sought approval and Reuben was happy to oblige.

"Mmmm, smells great and looks even better! Thank you, ma'am!"

"You're mighty welcome, my friend. If you need sumpin' else, just whistle!" she declared as she turned back to the kitchen.

Before he could start, Reuben was surprised by one of the men saying, "Careful stranger, you get too familiar with Ma, she'll hogtie you 'till the preacher comes an' you'll be married 'fore you know it!" he chuckled as he spoke.

171

Reuben turned to look at the men, saw a star on the speaker's chest, and said, "You the sheriff?"

"I am," answered the man, his chin whiskers bouncing as he spoke. "Why?"

Reuben motioned him to come to the table and both men rose, grabbed up their coffee cups and joined Reuben as he started whittling on his steak. He looked up at the sheriff, "I was a deputy for Sheriff Thorington out of Scott county," he paused as he took a big bite of steak, his stomach growling as he did, then added, "It was just special duty while I chased a bunch o' brigands callin' themselves the Home Guard. They had struck in Michigan and I followed them into Iowa. Finally caught up with 'em and stopped their doin's."

He took another bite of the juicy steak, washed it down with coffee, and looked at the sheriff. "But now, I'm on the trail of a bunch that's part of Captain Quantrill's Bushwhackers outa Missouri." He watched the sheriff getting a little antsy as he twisted in his seat, glancing at his friend. "They hit three farms today, the last one just north of here, couple hours ago, I think it was the Canterbury farm, judging by the grave markers."

The sheriff and his tobacco-stained chin whiskers sat back as if he had been hit. He looked at his friend whose droopy mustache hung below his chin and both men had eyes the size of saucers. They looked at Reuben as the sheriff asked, "You sure 'bout that farm?"

"I don't rightly know. All I had to go on was the grave markers, everything else was burning. The cows were dead in the corral and if there were any bodies, they were burnin', smelt like it anyway."

"North of here you say? 'bout how fer?" asked the skinny one with the mustache.

"'bout five miles."

The two looked at each other and started to rise but were stopped by Reuben, "Just a minute sheriff. I just stopped to give my horse a rest and to get some food," pointing at his plate with his fork, "and to let you know what was goin' on. Now, I plan on gettin' back on their trail soon's I'm done, so if you're wantin' to, you can join me. But I sent Sheriff Thorington his deputy badge back and I'm just doin' this cuz, well, somebody has to."

The sheriff looked at his deputy, "Demas, give him yore badge!" and turned to the door. He looked back at Reuben, "What's yore name, boy?"

"Reuben Grundy."

"You're deputized, Reuben. I'm goin' to the farm you said was burnin' cuz that's my brother's place. You catch them killers if you can, hang 'em if'n you want to, but they's all your'n!"

The lanky mustache hurried up to catch the sheriff and Reuben sat staring at the open door as Ma came to his side with a thick piece of apple pie. With one hand on her hip, glaring at the door, she asked, "Where them two off to?"

"Sheriff said he was goin' to his brother's farm north of here."

"Well, why on earth for? He usually sits there till suppertime."

"His brother's farm was hit by Bushwhackers and was burning when I came past."

Ma stepped back, eyebrows lifted and both hands on her hips. She slapped one hand to her mouth and muffled her words, "No! Can't be!"

"Ummhmmm," answered Reuben pulling the pie closer.

"You keep ridin' that horse like you been doin', you gonna kill 'im!" said the liveryman, standing at the stall of the sorrel. "Look at that lather," pointing at the wet brush, "an' the way he was breathin' you mighta winded him. What's so all fired important that you gotta kill a horse fer, anyway?"

"Some Missouri Bushwhackers been raidin' farms and killin' the families!" growled Reuben, looking around the livery. He frowned when he spotted the dark back of a horse above the boards of a stall toward the end of the livery. A dark head turned toward him, bright but soft eyes looking at him curiously. Reuben walked closer, leaned against the fence to look at the horse a little more closely, glanced back to the liveryman, "This'n for sale?"

"Hadn't thought about it," answered Whiskers.

Reuben sided the horse, ran his hand over his rump and down the legs, lifted one hoof and ran a hand under the animal's belly. The horse stood quiet, skin twitching slightly at his touch but never moving. He walked toward the horse's head, stroked his neck, ran his hand along his back, reached down and picked up a fore hoof and put it down. The horse was haltered and tied and Reuben loosed the lead rope, backed him out of the stall and walked him into the daylight. He stepped back for a better look. Standing fifteen-two, the blue roan stood proud and spirited. Reuben lifted the roan's head and looked at his teeth, judging him to be a good four years old. The blue roan had strong legs, short back, deep chest, and broad rump. He liked what he saw and looked back at Whiskers.

"What's your best price?"

Whiskers walked to Reuben's side, stroking his beard, spat some tobacco, and looked at Reuben, "I di'nt really wanna sell him. He's a good horse, he'll run all day, turn on a three-cent nickel and give you two Indian head pennies in change. He's the best horse I ever had even if he is an ugly color that no one wants," grumbled Whiskers.

"I also need a better saddle, that McClellan is givin' me blisters on my rear!"

Whiskers ran his fingers through his beard, snapped his braces, and said, "I gotta a good Hope Texas saddle, big tapaderos, saddlebags, the works."

"Twenty dollars for horse and saddle," offered Reuben.

Whiskers cocked his head to the side, shaking it slowly, "Cain't do it."

"Thirty dollars, and that'ns," nodding to the sorrel, "gear but not the sorrel, I'll be back for him."

Whiskers grinned, pulled his thumb from his braces, and stretched out his hand as he grinned broadly showing both teeth. He slapped his hand in Reuben's, "Done!"

Reuben was geared up in no time, stepped into the

new saddle and wiggled around in the seat, liking the feel of the full seat with cantle at the back and a good horn atop the pommel. The saddlebags were bigger and his bedroll rode well behind the cantle. He was pleased and when the big horse stretched out, it was obvious he was anxious to stretch his legs. Reuben was impressed at the smooth canter of the horse. *This is a horse you can ride all day and think you were at home in a rockin' chair,* thought Reuben, grinning, and enjoying the wind in his face. When they clattered across the covered bridge that stretched over the Weldon River, the shod hooves sounded like the parade drums of a cavalry and Reuben smiled again.

The trail of the raiders was easy to pick up, the tracks showed the six raiders were leading four loaded pack-horses and were moving at a fast walk. The deep tracks dug up the moist and grassy soil as they cut their own trail, still due south. Less than five miles south of Garden Grove, Reuben hit another crossroad with a sign that showed Leon to the west but the tracks of the raiders continued south. Still following the Weldon river that had farms on both sides, he expected to see another farm going up in smoke just any time.

––––––––

"Bob, you take Pickles and Bull, go 'round the barn and come through it to the house. I'll take the kid and Booger and we'll come at it at the front door, there past the well." Fletch Taylor was sitting his horse, pointing to the farm buildings as he gave orders to his men. He turned back, "Pickles, you tie off them packhorses then go with Bob here."

"Hehehe, sho'nuff Fletch!" cackled the skinny scalper.

He reined his mount around and slipped to the ground, accepting the lead lines from the others and tethered the four packhorses to the saplings, allowing enough lead for them to graze on the dry grass nearby. He swung back aboard and hurried to catch up with Bob and Bull. They stayed in the trees that bordered the cornfield, well back from the buildings, until they neared the back of the barn. Bob stopped, looking at the barn and other outbuildings for any workers, when Pickles asked, "Ain't this the last one?"

"Yeah, 'less he spots another'n 'fore we cross the border," answered Bob, quietly. He glanced to Bull then nudged his mount from the trees, pointing the three to the corral at the back of the barn. He had spotted four horses in the corral, their heads in the hay mow, munching contentedly. They tied off their mounts at the pole fence, climbed over with rifles in hand, and started through the barn. Two more horses with colts were in stalls next to a milk cow and each turned to look at the strange men coming into the barn. The bright sun at their backs made them appear as dark figures but the only alarm was from protective mares that pushed the nursing colts against the stall fencing.

Bull nodded toward the horses, spoke quietly, "We'll just take the ones in the corral. These mare'll give us too much trouble less'n we take the colts too, and they'd be trouble 'nuff."

"Hey! What're you doin' in our barn?" the words came from a youngster of about twelve but startled the three men. Bob started to answer when the whisper of the thrown Bowie knife passed his ear then buried itself in the chest of the boy, whose eyes flared with fear, his mouth opened but no sound came. The impact of the big knife dropping him instantly to the ground.

Bob snapped around to glare at Pickles, "I coulda talked to him!"

"Why? We can't leave nobody alive to talk about us, so . . ." replied Pickles as he shrugged, a grin splitting his face as he walked to the body to retrieve his knife.

Bob shook his head, nodded for the two to follow and started to the front of the big barn.

———

"HOWDY MISTER!" DECLARED FLETCH, AS HE SAT HIS HORSE before the farm house. The farmer was standing on the front stoop, a shotgun cradled in his arms as he shaded his eyes to look at the strangers in his yard.

"Howdy. What'chu want?"

"Well," started Fletch as he stood in his stirrups, looking around the farm. He glanced back to the barn and saw Bob standing at the edge of the big door, then turned back to face the farmer, "I guess you could say we want everything!" and chuckled as he grinned at the stunned man.

"What'chu mean, everything? This place ain't for sale," he answered, starting to lift the shotgun. But the blast from Booger's Enfield .58 stopped him when the minié ball took him in the sternum, dropping him in a heap on the stoop.

Fletch turned to Bull in the doorway of the barn, "Get the horses an' burn it!" He turned to Booger, motioned to the house and both Booger and Jesse dropped to the ground and started for the house. Fletch reined around to look over the out buildings, searching for anything of value or use, and spotted a farm wagon. He turned and hollered to Bull, "Hey Bull! Any harness in there for a team to pull a wagon?"

"No, but there's four horses in the corral!"

"Get 'em and bring 'em here!" answered Fletch as he stepped down to push open the door of a two-room shed. The first room had saddles and harness hanging from the rafters and pegs on the wall and he started sorting out a set of harness for a team. His idea was to use the wagon so they could carry more plunder but only if needed. He tossed the harness outside, then opened the door to the second room, saw it was a smoke house sealed off from the tack shed and it was full of hams, loins, quarters, and more. He grinned at the bounty, knowing this was the best haul of all the farms they took so far. This was what Captain Quantrill wanted, provisions for the hungry men of his growing company. He chuckled as he started to lift one of the quarters from its hook but was startled by the blast of gunfire and the shouts of his men.

He turned back to the door but carefully looked about for the source of the shooting and shouting and saw the inert form of Booger lying just outside the front door of the house. He frantically began searching for anyone with a weapon but, seeing no one, started to step from the shed, only to hear another blast that came from the barn as Bob returned fire on a target almost two hundred yards away in the same trees they came from to approach the farm. Someone was in those trees, but who? The only ones they spotted were already dead, the farmer and anyone in the house. He hugged the edge of the doorway, looking at the trees, refusing to make himself a target. He glanced toward the house, saw Jesse moving at the rear of the house, looking toward him, motioning toward the trees.

He looked to the barn, saw movement in the loft and recognized Pickles looking his way and motioning toward the trees. He shook his head, *both these idjits think I don't know there's somebody in the trees shooting at us.* He ducked back inside the shed, tried to see out of a knot hole and still did not see any movement in the trees. He saw Jesse at the back of the house, waving to get his attention, but he wasn't about to step into the doorway just to signal the kid. *Whoever that is sure has us pinned down.* He looked out the knot hole again, turned to look at the doorway to the smoke room, and had a thought. With a glance to the doorway, he moved to the door of the smoke room, stepped through, and went to the back wall.

He grinned as he looked at the weathered and smoky boards and began kicking at the longest ones in the middle of the back wall. The sound carried and seemed to echo but he kept at it, knowing this was the only way to get out of sight of the shooter. His horse was standing ground tied between the house and shed and in clear view of the shooter. His rifle was in the scabbard and all he had was the Colt Paterson revolver behind his belt. He kept kicking at the loosened board, kicked it free and started on the one next to it. But then what?

R euben rode wary, watching for any change in the direction of travel of the raiders, knowing the slightest change could signal another attack. When the river made a bend to the west, angling off east of a nearby timber-covered bluff, the tracks of the raiders turned toward the timber. They had been keeping to the trees beside the river, but a finger of thick brush and trees split a pair of cornfields and the tracks followed the finger. Reuben reined up, stood in his stirrups for a look see and with nothing alarming, pushed into the thickets close on the trail of the raiders. He absentmindedly reached for his Sharps, limbering it in the scabbard, and with the Henry as well. At the point of the finger, a stretch of open land split the thickets and Reuben stopped. Looking around, he used the time to check the loads in both rifles and satisfied, pushed across the stretch to take to the timber that shouldered a long bluff.

To the east of the bluff, on Reuben's left side, a wide field showed corn stubble and across the field, a farm-house, barn, and other outbuildings showed a well-established farm, just the kind of target that appealed to the Bushwhackers. He reined up as he saw riders coming from the trees at the far end of the field, moving toward the barn. A little further, three more rode the edge of the trees, apparently making for the house. Reuben knew they were about to strike and he nudged the roan into the trees that faced the farmhouse. He stepped down, slapped the reins around a branch of a sycamore and, with the Sharps in hand, moved to the edge of the trees. A quick glance showed he was shy of two hundred yards from the house and he lifted the binoculars that hung at his neck for a better look.

There were six of the Bushwhackers, three moving to the barn, three to the house, and Reuben knew he could not take them all on in a stand-alone fight but maybe he could even the odds a little, hopefully, save some of the farmer's family. He chose a big hickory, leaned against the shaggy bark and watched the men approach the farm. Three men, all mounted, sat before the house and a man came to the stoop, holding a rifle. It looked harmless enough and Reuben had a passing thought that these might not be the Bushwhackers, maybe someone else that meant no harm. But the sudden blast of a rifle from one of the mounted men verified his suspicions as the farmer crumpled to the ground.

Reuben lowered the glasses, lifted the Sharps, and eared back the hammer, setting the double triggers. A quick glance reassured him of the percussion cap in place and he watched as two of the men entered the house, the third appearing to holler at those in the barn. Reuben steadied his breathing, his nostrils flaring and his tension mounting as it always did when he was readying a shot. This was what he had become accustomed to with Berdan's Sharpshooters whenever he was sent on a mission. The killer instinct rose to the fore and his nerves calmed, a dead calm like still waters over a deep pool, nothing twitching, nothing moving, breath coming steady, eyes narrowing to slits. He had a sight picture down the long tube of the scope and he waited. It was but a few moments until a big man stepped from the house, took a long step over the body of the farmer and Reuben squeezed off his shot.

The big Sharps barked and bucked, the boom echoing across the open field and the lead bullet flew true, striking the big man in the low chest, to the right of the sternum, and exploding out his back, taking a double fist-sized chunk of bone and flesh with it as it splashed blood and slime over the door. Reuben instantly lowered the Sharps and quickly moved about fifteen feet further down the tree line, taking cover behind a tall but naked white oak. Without hesitation, he reloaded the Sharps and was almost instantly ready for another shot but he lifted his binoculars to watch the movement of the Bush-whackers.

The front of the house was almost directly in line with his position but the front of the barn was at a slight angle. He could see behind and beyond the house to the other outbuildings and saw the horse of one of the men standing between the house and the bigger of the sheds. A flash of movement showed a man at the door of the shed but he quickly ducked back as a rifle boomed at the front of the barn. Reuben knew the shot was a feeler, for they had no way of knowing where he was and only guessed where he had been. He watched the front of the barn, saw a big man peering out at the big door, then movement revealed a man at the loft. The one in the loft was less than careful and was waving toward the man in the shed.

Reuben chuckled as he slowly lifted the Sharps and

narrowed his scope sight on the figure in the loft. He breathed deep, let it out and steadied his stance against the oak and started his squeeze. It was a little less than two hundred yards, an easy shot for Reuben, and he brought pressure on the thin trigger. The Sharps bucked as it spat grey smoke and lead, sending the .52 caliber ball on its way. Reuben peered through the thinning smoke, watching the target in the loft tumble from the opening, his chest blossoming red, and twist as he fell head first onto the hard ground below, dead.

Reuben was on the move almost before the one known as Pickles fell from the loft and Reuben had jacked open the breech as he reached for another cartridge. He was moving back to his left, past his first position, as he slipped the next cartridge into the breech and jacked it closed. He grabbed a cap from his possibles bag and slipped it onto the nipple, crimping it with his calloused fingertips. A big silver maple offered what he needed and he dropped to one knee behind the big tree, looked at the farm yard and lifted the binoculars. His new position gave him a slightly better angle on the barn and he searched the big building for another target. Suddenly, rifle fire erupted from the barn and beside the house. Both were rifles but a pistol also spoke from near the bigger of the outbuildings.

Reuben knew they had no idea of his position but even a blind squirrel can find a nut once in a while and he leaned back behind the maple, knowing they would be moving and the gunfire was to keep his head down while they moved and maybe score a lucky shot.

———

FLETCH MADE IT OUT OF THE SMOKE HOUSE, USED IT FOR cover and moved beside the barn, keeping it between him and the shooter. He looked back toward the house, hollered at Jesse, "Hey kid! When I start shooting, take a couple shots then get your horse and come behind these sheds!" He turned toward the front of the barn, "Bob, Bull, when I start shooting, you open up on the trees and the shooter. It'll cover for the kid as he comes around and for me to get in the barn."

He gave them but a moment, then lifted his Paterson revolver and cut loose. When the others opened fire, he hesitated just a moment, then ducked and ran into the barn just moments before Jesse ducked into the back door. The kid looked up at Fletch, "My horse is by the corral," motioning to the back.

"Good," replied Fletch as he dropped to the dirt beside the first stall. He shook his head as Bull and Bob came near, looked up at them, "Can you see where he is?"

"Nope, but he's in the trees yonder, same place we come from," growled Bull.

"How we gonna get outa here?" asked Bob, breathing heavily as he dropped to one knee beside Fletch.

"We're gonna fire the buildings, let the fire and smoke cover us. But my horse is still between the house and the sheds, so, after we light the barn, the three of you will give me cover, and the kid can fire the sheds while I get my horse and fire the house."

"We gonna get them horses outa the corral?"

"Yeah, and there's a bunch of meat we need outa that shed I was in, so, we can use the barn for cover first, get to the back of the shed and load up some meat. Then I'll get my horse when you fire the barn, and we'll skedaddle out behind the barn and such. The shooter's on the other side of the field in the trees and can't get to us behind the barn and with the fire goin' he won't know when we shag it outa here."

"The only place we can shoot from is the big door there," started Bob, nodding to the front door of the barn, "and he done kilt Pickles up in the loft."

"You got a better idea?" asked Fletch, cocking one eyebrow up as he glared at the man.

Bob looked at Bull, "You wanna shoot or get the horses and load meat?"

"I'll get the horses," grunted the big man, rising to his feet and turning to the back door of the barn. The two mares and colts were still in their stalls and he looked at them as he passed, then opened the stalls and drove the horses out of the barn before him. He glanced back at the others, "They'll make him look and you can get a better shot at him," he declared, grinning as if he had a bright idea they did not understand. As he approached the back door, he looked back to the others to await the signal from Fletch for the action to begin.

Movement at the back of the barn caught Reuben's attention as the horses were milling about, skittish about something. He watched two mares with colts by their side slide along the fence rail, looking over their shoulders at something. A big man, trying unsuccessfully to stay low, moved among the horses, trying to halter them. The six horses and two colts were stirring up a dust cloud as they ran back and forth, avoiding the man, and bumping one another about. Reuben took aim at the corral. He was hesitant to take a shot and hit a horse but the other men were sheltered in the barn. The corner of the corral that was obscured by the barn was put to use by the man as he caught one of the horses, tethering it in the corner, then started for another.

Reuben's gaze moved from the front to the back of the barn, watching for a possible shot, when gunfire erupted, and bullets started whizzing through the trees and brush nearby. He moved behind the big tree, just as a bullet tore a piece of bark within inches of his shoulder, crowding him further. He was certain they had not seen him and were randomly shooting at the tree line but that one came mighty close. A sudden scream and whinny from the trees behind him made him move deeper into the woods, fearful of the roan having taken a bullet. But the horse still stood complacent, unconcerned about the ruckus and appeared hipshot and asleep until Reuben reached out to stroke his neck, "You alright, Blue? Was that you that made that noise?"

The sound of hooves on dry leaves dropped Reuben to one knee, looking about the thick woods for approaching horses, but the footfalls were random, uneven, and he thought it might be tethered horses. He slowly rose and began to stealthily move deeper into the trees toward the sounds and, when a horse blew, he spotted the four packhorses, standing tethered in a bit of a clearing. He looked around. He knew these had been left behind by the raiders, but he doubted they would try to return for them. He stepped close, quickly loosened the girths of the pack saddles, and returned to the tree line to watch the raiders.

The horse behind the house was gone, the dust was settling in the corral behind the barn, but he saw no other movement until motion showed in the narrow walkway between the shed and the barn. A led horse passed behind the shed, and Reuben lifted the Sharps, sighting through the scope, waiting for more movement. When another horse passed the walkway, he saw the man leading the animal was on the far side, using the horse as a shield and he could not take the quick shot. He waited.

Flames showed in the window of the farmhouse but he could not see any of the men until he noticed a flash of movement near the smaller shed behind the house. With the scope mounted to the side of the barrel of the

Sharps, he also had the ladder sight and front blade sight which he focused on, keeping his eyes on the entire farmyard for any sign of the men. The raiders were being cautious, knowing to show themselves would draw lead. Reuben's eyes flashed back and forth, catching the slightest motion and flames began to blossom behind the sheds, then movement. He had already eared back the hammer and set the triggers, when a big man started from the barn, stumbling as he looked back at fast-growing flames. Reuben squeezed off his shot. The bullet struck Bull just below his ear and blasted out the other side of his face and neck, spinning the man into the ground like a twisted corkscrew. The sound of the blast echoed back from the barn, but the big barn had erupted in flames, making the combined fires from the house, sheds and barn flare like a forest fire, smoke spiraling up like a funnel cloud of a tornado. Horses were screaming, the two mares at the back corral breaking through the fence and urging their colts to follow. Spindly legs picked their way through the broken poles and slats, bounded to their mothers and the four fled to the trees beyond the fields. The bellow of a milk cow was quickly silenced amid the crashing timbers. Reuben watched, shaking his head, anger bringing bile to his throat.

He knew the men would try to flee behind the smokescreen and he went to his horse. He had already reloaded the Sharps, and slid it into the scabbard, stuffed his foot in the tapadero and swung aboard, "All right, Blue, time to show your stuff! Their horses are gonna be tired; they been moving quick all day so we can catch 'em if you stretch out!" He started to move out when a whinny from the trees told him of the other horses. He thought he would come back for them depending on his chase of the raiders yet, not willing to chance it, he reined the roan into the trees to free the tethered horses and let them find their way to feed and water. He dug heels to the blue to explode from the trees toward the thickets by the river where he expected to pick up the trail of the Bushwhackers.

Giving the flaming farm a wide berth, Reuben crashed through the thickets at river's edge, splashed into the water and crossed the shallow stream in bounds. When the roan climbed the far bank, Reuben brought him to a standstill as he sat listening and watching. Just beyond the line of the underbrush, the edge of a farm field was dug up with hoof prints. He dropped to one knee, examining the tracks, imprinting them in his mind, and swung back aboard. "Let's go Blue!"

The big roan humped his back as he brought his hind feet under his belly to launch them on the path of the murderers. Reuben's survey of the tracks showed the remaining three were trailing the four packhorses, at least two of them loaded, and they were on the run. But when the blue roan stretched out, his nose in the wind, mane and tail flying like a three-masted schooner, the ground swept beneath them. The area farms had been laid out in a similar fashion to the eastern farms, hedgerows dividing the fields more often than fences but the fleeing bandits showed no mercy on their mounts and crashed through the brush and trees, desperate to put distance between them and their pursuer.

The roan never faltered in his stride; well rested and grain fed, he obviously was enjoying the run and within moments, the dust and tails of the raiders' horses were seen smashing through the next hedgerow. The blue seemed to stretch out further and faster, Reuben laying low on the gelding's neck, mane slapping his face, but the regular breathing of the horse told his rider the big blue was enjoying his run.

They were steadily gaining on the raiders when the trailing one turned, spotted their hunter, and shouted to the others. The skinny one to the far right twisted in his saddle and fired a revolver but Reuben saw nothing but a slight puff of smoke. He heard the muffled blast of the shot but felt nor heard anything else. The big man in the back of the pack was trailing two horses, neither with a saddle, and he threw the lead ropes in the air and ducked low on his horse's neck as the two led horses veered off to the side, slowing their pace.

The two men in the lead still trailed loaded pack-horses and the third man, unhindered with the other horses, was gaining on them, but his mount was lathered, tired, and struggling for breath. Their horses had been moving fast all day, the raids on farms the only time they stopped, and all were slowing and struggling. The thunder of hooves gave Reuben the thought he was riding through a black storm cloud with the thunder rolling beneath foretelling of the coming storm. But the blue was only concerned about the race and knew he was gaining and seemed to increase his pace, bringing him close to the big man.

Reuben slipped the Henry from the scabbard, jacked a round into the chamber and laid the barrel across his elbow as he drew close. The big man looked over his right shoulder at Reuben, his eyes flared, and he turned to shout at the others. Reuben shrugged his left arm forward and squeezed off his shot. The big man looked at Reuben, fear in his eyes as he gasped for breath, slumped, and tumbled from his saddle, his horse slowing as he was freed of his rider.

The other raiders slapped legs to the sides of their

tired horses, loosed the lead ropes of the packhorses, and twisted in their saddles to take potshots at the man behind them. Reuben felt a branding sear at his side, jammed the Henry back into the scabbard and slowed the blue to a walk. He felt at his side, bringing his hand back covered with blood, and felt the stabbing pain of a bullet wound. He shook his head and brought the blue to a stop, opened his jacket, and lifted his linen shirt to see the bloody bullet hole in his side. He looked up to see the two raiders disappear over a slight rise and shook his head, knowing his chase was finished.

He reined the blue to the riverbank, stepped down and scooped up a clump of mud and moss, twisted around to pack the front and back of the bullet hole and, with a length of rope from his saddlebags, he tied his shirt tight around the wound to stabilize the mudpack, and stepped back aboard the blue. "Let's go fetch them horses, maybe get the dead man and take him back to the sheriff," he was talking to his horse like men alone are wont to do but he chuckled at the thought and reached down to stroke Blue's neck, realizing he had already named the animal. He smiled as he lifted his eyes to search for the packhorses and the others.

————

HE DREW A LOT OF ATTENTION AS HE RODE INTO THE little settlement of Garden Grove. Folks came from the emporium and taverns to gawk at the stranger with a bloody side, trailing two loaded packhorses, one saddle horse with a body draped over the saddle, and two other horses. Reuben was tired. Tired from the fight, the chase, and from loss of blood, and when he reined up in front of the sheriff's office, he slid from his saddle, leaned against the horse a moment, then tethered the roan. He stepped up to the boardwalk and staggered into the sheriff's office to slump into a chair beside the desk. He looked from under the brim of his floppy felt hat, grinned at the sheriff, and asked, "You got a doctor in this town?"

The sheriff motioned to the lanky deputy with the droopy mustache and turned to Reuben, "Looks like you caught one of 'em."

"Ummhmm, you'll find three more at the farm south of here. The one at the bend of the river. The buildings were still smokin' when I came back by, don't know how many folks they kilt 'fore I got there. But . . . two of 'em got away, prob'ly in Missouri by now." He dropped his head to his arms that lay crossed on the sheriff's desk, then mumbled, "I'd still be after 'em if I hadn't taken this bullet," and lost consciousness where he sat.

"That horse belongs to a friend of mine and I'm takin' it back," began Reuben, nodding to the little sorrel as he talked with Whiskers at the livery. "Don't rightly know what the sheriff will do with these other'ns and there's four more out to that farm south of here the Bushwhackers hit. I think the sheriff went after those cuz they're loaded with plunder. I reckon he thinks there might be some of his brother's stuff among the packs but you might talk to him 'bout the horses."

"I dunno, that sheriff, he don't cotton to me much. Hehehe, I got the better of 'im on a horse trade onct an' he ain't 'bout to ferget it! Hehehe, stick aroun' a day or two an' I'll tell ya' 'bout it!" declared Whiskers, slapping his leg, and snapping his braces. He was grinning his mostly toothless smile while excess tobacco juice dribbled through his whiskers. "Kinda hate to see you go, young'un, we ain't had so much excitement roun' chere in a long time!" He slapped his leg again, almost choked on his tobacco and spat out a plug. He stood beside the big door, watching Reuben lead his blue roan and the little sorrel out of the livery.

"If yer' wantin' to catch up to yer frien's 'fore they cross the Missoura, head due west from chere," he pointed to the bridge across the Weldon River, "an' you'll hit the Big Muddy. If you're lucky, ya' can ketch a river-boat or keelboat goin' north and get to the big crossin' 'fore they does!"

"Might just do that," answered Reuben as he swung aboard his blue roan. "And thanks for Blue here, he's a good 'un!"

"Treat 'im right!" declared Whiskers, stepping away from the horses. He held a hand in a wave as Reuben started back down the main street of Garden Grove. One more stop and he would be on his way, even though the sun was slowly disappearing beyond the western horizon and was saying good night with a glorious display of red-bottomed clouds and great shafts of orange and red scratching at the darkening sky. He reined up at Ma's eats, stepped down and slapped the reins of Blue and the lead rope of the little sorrel over the hitch rail, and walked into the eatery. He was greeted by Ma with a broad smile and a pair of tow sacks full of goodies cradled in her arms. "If I was a man, I'd swear! So help me, when I heard what those Bushwhackers did to those farmers, I wanted to light out after 'em my own self! But I be thanking God He sent you here to catch up to 'em; He knows ain't nobody roun' here would be doin' nothin' 'bout it!" she glared at the sheriff and deputy sitting at their usual table.

Reuben chuckled, "Now Ma, they didn't even know those Bushwhackers were in the area, much less what they were up to," he spoke as he walked to the sheriff's table. He reached into his shirt pocket, extracted the deputy badge, and lay it before the lanky deputy, who grinned and nodded as he reached out to pick up the badge. Reuben turned back to Ma, "Sides, Ma, if there had been too many of us, we'd been shootin' each other!" He stepped closer to Ma as she held out the sacks, "What'chu got for me?" as he started to open the first sack but was stopped when Ma slapped his hand. "It's a surprise. You just wait till you get good and hungry and stop to eat, then you'll be thinking kindly of Ma!"

"Then give me a hug that I won't forget!" declared Reuben as he smiled mischievously at the portly woman. He opened his arms wide, and she stepped close, pulling him closer as she hugged him tightly. When she loosened her grip, he stepped back, gasping, smiling, and laughing. "Ma, you are unforgettable!"

She laughed as her cheeks reddened and she grabbed a hanky from her apron pocket, "Oh, you say that to all the girls!" and dabbed at her eyes.

Reuben chuckled, turned away as he tipped his hat, nodded to the sheriff, and stepped through the door. The full moon was already showing its silvery face in the eastern sky, even though dusk was still offering ample light for traveling. Reuben stepped aboard Blue and reined away from the hitchrail, clucked, and nudged the roan, drew the lead line to the halter of the sorrel taut, and rode from the little settlement.

When he crossed the bridge, he remembered the last time the staccato of hooves echoed back and he heaved a heavy sigh, let a slight grin tug at the corner of his mouth, and let the pictured memory of Claire and little Charlie lead him onward. The terrain had become monotonous but the fading light of dusk offered different views; the hills became shadows, swales were lakes of black, trees became skeletal silhouettes. While the sounds of night were comforting; the deep-throated strumming of loons on the many ponds, the crickets and cicadas clattering their rhythmic rattles, bullfrogs competing for their lily pads, and owls asking their endless questions, it was more the rhythmic gait of his mount that gave him a reassurance of the presence of a friend and companion in his big blue roan. But the haunting cacophony of the trickster coyotes and their occasional rendezvous questions asked of the darkness that echoed unanswered and added to the loneliness of the darkness.

Reuben settled into the comforting gait of the blue roan and occasionally talked to Blue like a traveling companion, asking questions in the moonlight that met with nothing more than a twitch of an ear or at most a turn of his head as the roan looked at his rider from the corner of his eye, usually just before a slight nod of the head. But the two were growing close, developing the bond between man and horse that would become greater than that of best friends.

He remembered the advice of Whiskers about traveling due west and that the first river crossing would be about midnight when he had to cross the Thompson. "It ain't much but it'll get'chu wet if ye ain't careful!" were the words of caution the whiskery old man gave. Reuben chuckled at the memory and also remembered he said there were "half-doz'n or so more cricks 'n rivers ye git to wade fer ya' get to the Big Muddy."

After traveling for several miles, he glanced at the constellation of Ursa Major, what some were calling the Big Dipper, and guessed it to be close to midnight. In the distance across the rolling flats, he saw the rumpled black line that appeared to indicate the trees and such along a river bank. As he moved nearer, what he had seen as a river bank was the river low down in a deep depression, the thirty-foot banks covered with brush

197

and stubby trees. Several taller trees stood nearer the water's edge and the big moon gave enough light that he spotted a trail to the bottom and nudged the blue to take the trail. Once at river's edge, Reuben stepped down, loosened the girth on the blue and led both horses to the water, then picketed them on some nearby grass, still showing green in the moonlight.

He found a seat at the base of a mature black willow and opened the first tow sack from Ma. She had stuffed the bag with biscuits, slices of roast beef, a container of strawberry jam, and a whole apple pie. He gathered a few dry sticks to make enough of a fire for some coffee and soon had the hat-sized fire flaring. With the small pot at the side of the flames, his cup at his side, he knew it would be ready about the time he finished his meal. He shook his head happily as he lay out what he would have for his midnight meal, set the bag aside, and leaned back to enjoy his repast.

He popped the last of the biscuit in his mouth and reached for the coffee pot when a voice out of the darkness said, "Do you have food to share?" Reuben stopped his move, carefully turned his head to the side as he looked into the darkness with squinted eyes, he spotted a leathery face showing in the firelight. And a man stepped forward, a blanket over his shoulders, his greying hair in braids under the blanket, and his dark skin showing deep black eyes shadowed by wrinkles. He was a lean man, native, with moccasins and hide britches, but a friendly smile and laughing eyes. "I am Appanoose, son of Taimah, son of Quashquame, of the Meskwaki people. May I join you?"

Reuben sat back, nodded, "Welcome, and yes, I have food to share." With a glance at the man, he reached into the sack and brought out a pair of biscuits, slapped some roast beef on them, and handed them to his visitor. "I am Reuben Grundy, on my way to the Missouri River to meet up with friends."

The man nodded, accepted the biscuits, and began to eat. "I too travel to the Big Muddy. I wish to see more of this great land before I die. My son, Kesheska, has taken my place as chief of the Meskwaki, and I choose to travel in my later years."

"But you're walking, and at night, I don't understand," asked Reuben, frowning.

"You too are traveling at night. What is there to understand?"

Reuben chuckled, shook his head slightly, "Well, winter's coming, it's colder, you don't seem to have much, and, well, you're not too young."

The old man smiled, continuing with his feast, "The land has always provided all that I need. And there are many good people that I meet, like you, that are willing to share. When I have much to share, I am always willing to give to others."

It was only then as the man leaned forward to accept a cup of coffee that Reuben noticed he had a bow and quiver at his back and assumed the man also had a knife and perhaps more. Reuben chuckled, "Well, since we're both going to the river and I just happen to have an extra horse, perhaps you would like to join me for the journey?"

As Reuben tightened the girth on the saddle aboard the roan, he glanced to the Indian who stood at the head of the sorrel, stroking the horse's face and neck, talking in low tones, letting the animal sniff and nuzzle him. Reuben smiled, knowing he could learn from this man. He checked his gear, secured the toe sacks, and swung aboard. He watched the old man as he stood beside the sorrel and, in practiced moves, the man, with a handful of mane, hopped up, bellied down over the back of the sorrel, swung a leg over the rump and sat up. Reuben nodded and started out into the water to cross the Thompson River.

They had ridden for about an hour when the trail widened and Appanoose came alongside. "So, tell me about your people, Appanoose," suggested Reuben. They were on an easy road that pointed due west, the full moon casting long shadows of the leafless trees across the roadway; the night had grown still and the men sided one another.

As Appanoose began to talk, he dropped the lead of

the sorrel to the gelding's neck and began to speak, using sign language with his spoken English. "My people have been peaceful for many years but, before the English came, we fought with the French before we were driven from our homeland. Because of the trade, many learned both French and English to talk with the traders and our enemies. It was the black robes that taught us their tongue as they tried to make us take their religion."

"In my father's time, we came from the northeast into the land now called Iowa and made our home. Our people made bark lodges and brush huts and grew much of our food. We traded for horses, and our people bred them, and our herds increased. When the English came, they drove us further from our homes and we fought beside the Americans against the English. Because of this, when the American President, Andrew Jackson, demanded the native peoples be removed, many of our people were forced southwest to reservations but some stayed and the leaders of Iowa made it a law that we could buy land and live in Iowa in a place named after my father, Tama. My people live in Tama now, but many Meskwaki were moved to the southwest beyond the Big Muddy. I go to see them, and if I live, I will see more of the land to the west."

He continued to use sign as he spoke, his hands and fingers moving fluently almost as if he were drawing the words in the air. He paused, looking at Reuben, "When we grow old and are of no use to the people, we often go away to be alone when we meet our Creator."

"Why do you speak with your hands as you talk?" asked Reuben, who had watched every motion and sign as they let the horses have their heads to walk on the moonlit trail.

Appanoose grinned, "It is for you to learn. Where you go, there will be many other people and most will not know your English but the language of sign is used by many. It may be different in some ways but, when you learn the language of the hands, you will speak with many people and understand what they say."

Reuben frowned, realizing that he was already recognizing many of the signs, knowing that most were basic in their form, often pointing to what was meant or signing what one would do to speak with others that did not know their language. If anyone thought of the sun, it was natural to make a circle, look at the sky, and shade one's eyes. Simply done, easily understood. He nodded, "It is good, I can understand why it would be helpful to know the sign. But we will be together but a few days. Is it possible to learn so much in such a short time?"

"I began to learn sign as a child while I learned French and English. Other tribes I knew as a young man, such as the Dakota, Kickapoo and others use the sign. I have used sign all my life and I learn more every time I use it."

As fellow travelers are prone to do, they spoke long and of many topics, each learning from the other. They crossed several creeks on their journey, some that had signs calling them rivers, and saw a few signs showing the direction and distance to settlements, the last one was for Mt. Ayr, and after crossing the Little Platte River that was more of a creek, they came to a sign showing Bedford, three miles south. This part of the country was little different than what they had already crossed but was less settled. There were farms but few that were well established, and most were still in the clearing stage, making fields out of wilderness that had little more than trees and brush.

The sun was showing color that stretched overhead, warning of its soon rising, when they saw the signs of another river before them and Reuben suggested, "Bout time for some rest and a pot of coffee. Sound alright to you?"

"Yes, the horses and their riders could use some rest also," replied Appanoose, grinning.

"I think you're right about that," Reuben started as they neared the river crossing which was a gravel bottomed shallow with a sign that said, *East Fork One Hundred and Two River.* He shook his head as he read the sign, wondering how they came up with a name like that but his stomach growled its indifference to the sign and Reuben responded as he pushed the roan across the shallows, found a clearing behind some willows and stepped down.

He stripped the gear from the roan, gave the horse a rubdown with some dry grasses, saw Appanoose doing the same for the sorrel and, when the man offered to picket both horses, Reuben acquiesced. He started gathering some wood for a fire to make coffee and maybe heat up some of Ma's offerings. He had the fire going and the coffee on and was digging out some biscuits when Appanoose came from the river's edge with two nice sized bass impaled on a single arrow, one still flopping. He had a big smile on his face as he held out the arrow to Reuben, who laughed, and slipped the fish off the shaft.

Reuben lay them on the log beside the fire, slipped his big Bowie from the scabbard and began to gut and behead the fish while Appanoose fetched a couple willow withes to hang the fish over the fire. When he returned, smiling, he said, "The Creator provides for us if we but look."

"Yes He does," answered Reuben, putting the fish on the sticks, and planting them beside the fire. The coffeepot was beginning to dance on the rock and Reuben scooped up a handful of grounds and dropped them into the boiling water. Within moments, the breakfast was ready and the men sat back to enjoy as the sun brought the blue back to the sky and warmth to the beginning of the day. With the meal finished, Reuben doused the fire with water, moved into the shade and spread out his blankets. With a nod to Appanoose who was already stretched out on his blanket, he lay back, pulled his hat over his eyes, and dozed off.

It was just after mid-day when the splash of water and the clatter of hooves on rocks brought Reuben instantly awake and upright. He stood up under the big oak, glanced to where Appanoose had been but the Indian, blanket and sorrel was nowhere to be seen. Reuben stepped from under the oak to see five mounted young men turn his direction and move close in to the clearing where he stood. He had slept in his frock uniform coat that now hung open, giving him ready access to his pistol and Bowie if either was needed and he crossed his arms loosely, allowing his right hand to rest unseen on the butt of the Remington revolver.

"Howdy!" he declared as the riders stopped, the apparent leader leaning forward with his arms crossed on the pommel of his saddle. Reuben noted that all of them were no more than boys, the oldest maybe sixteen, but even boys can be dangerous.

"Who are you and what are you doin' here?" the leader demanded, growling, and doing his best to look intimidating, but a quick glance from the young man beside him showed surprise at the leader's demands.

Reuben guessed the speaker was the leader only because he was the biggest of the bunch.

Reuben answered calmly, "If I thought it was any of your business, I'd tell you. But since what I do is of no concern to you, well . . ." shrugging and smiling at the young man.

The leader sat up, "We are the Southern Border Brigade, and your business is our business, so speak up and be quick about it!"

"You're a bit north of the border aren't you?" asked Reuben, still smiling and standing with feet apart, arms crossed.

"I'm gonna ask you one more time and if I don't get a straight answer we'll hang you from that tree yonder!" The man-sized boy was sitting tall in the saddle, had raised his voice, and was motioning with a stiff finger to emphasize his words.

"You are neither the law nor the army. You're just a bunch of volunteers that probably couldn't make it in the regular army and now you think you're somethin' special, so, uhuh, and if you know what's good for you, you'll scoot on down that road and keep on goin'," suggested Reuben, still smiling.

The leader bailed off his horse and stomped toward Reuben, grabbing at his waist for his pistol but when he started to lift it, he was staring down the one-eyed Remington in Reuben's hand. "Drop it!" growled Reuben, unwavering, but no longer smiling.

The leader froze when he saw the pistol aimed at his face and slowly stretched his arm to his side and dropped his own pistol to the ground. He began to stammer, his voice now an octave higher and squeaky, "Uh, we didn't mean nuthin'; we heard there was some Bushwhackers comin' crost the border and thought you might be one." He never took his eyes off the pistol in Reuben's hand as sweat drops began to show on his forehead.

Reuben glared at the youth but he caught movement from one of the others. One of the older boys sitting at the edge of the group had started to bring his rifle to bear on Reuben when an arrow whispered from the trees and impaled itself on the pommel of his saddle, causing him to drop the rifle and wet himself.

Reuben motioned with his pistol for the leader to back up, "Now mount up!" he ordered.

"But what about my pistol?" whined the embarrassed leader.

"You lost it!" answered Reuben, motioning again with his Remington for the youth to mount up. Once he was seated and picked up the reins from the horse's neck, Reuben spoke, "The Bushwhackers, at least one bunch of them, most of 'em are dead. You can check with Sheriff Canterbury at Garden Grove about them. Now, what you need to know is I've worked with Sheriff Thorington over in Scott County, Sheriff Hine in Muscatine County, and Sheriff Canterbury. I've chased down and killed a bunch callin' themselves the Home Guard, and that bunch of outlaws that were part of Captain Quantrill's Bushwhackers. So, I don't have time for a bunch of wannabe soldiers like the bunch of you that ran off from your mama's kitchen. Now, go on and get outa here 'fore I take you all down and paddle your behinds like a bunch of spoiled children!" He paused, watching the group look at one another, "Now, git!" he demanded with a wave of his pistol. The entire bunch jerked the heads of their horses around and dug heels to their ribs causing the horses to lunge and kick clods of dirt as they left at a run.

Appanoose walked from the trees, leading the sorrel and chuckling, asked, "Friends of yours?"

Reuben laughed, shaking his head, and turned to the roan to saddle up so they could put some miles behind them just in case the recalcitrant band of boys decided to return for some more mischief.

The sign was in the shape of a large arrow, whitewashed, with red letters, *Plattsmouth Ferry.* Reuben had drawn up, sat loosely in his saddle, and glanced at Appanoose, then turned his gaze on the wide and muddy river. It was almost two days since their confrontation with the self-appointed Border Guard, and their travel had been without incident. He looked at his weathered friend, "Well, Appanoose, here we are." He nodded to the water, "That's the Big Muddy and I'm supposed to meet my friends somewhere around here, but . . ." he stood in his stirrups, looking up and down the bank of the river but the only life that showed was the dozing ferryman who was snoozing under a big oak, his hat over his eyes.

A log cabin stood at the edge of the trees, a long porch covering the front and shading the door and windows, two wicker-bottomed rocking chairs sat empty but the door was invitingly open. It was only on the second glance that Reuben noticed a small sign hanging on the porch railing offering *Mickelwait Ferry*

Office, Supplies inside. He glanced to Appanoose, motioned to the store front, "Let's check there," and nudged the roan to the hitchrail. He stepped down, hung Blue's rein over the rail and mounted the steps to the porch to enter the cabin.

Pausing in the doorway for his eyes to adjust, Reuben casually rested his hand on the butt of his pistol until he noticed a grey-haired woman behind a short counter, smiling and nodding as she spoke, "Welcome! Lookin' to cross the river, are ye?"

Reuben stepped closer, doffed his hat and glanced around at the meager goods on the counter and few shelves, "Yes'm, and maybe get some information if I might."

"Just the two of you and your horses?" she asked, bending to the side to look out the fly-specked window and open doorway.

"Yes'm."

"Four bits. Say, ain't that a injun you got with you?"

"Yes'm."

She frowned, looking at Reuben with a critical eye, but apparently liked what she saw and smiled, "Well, I reckon we'll allow it this time. Them folks o'er in Plattsmouth don't like us lettin' injuns cross o'er, but . . ." she held out her hand awaiting payment as she smiled at Reuben. The broad smile showed tobacco-stained teeth, what there were of them, and wrinkles that folded on themselves as she smiled.

Reuben grinned as he dug out a half-dollar and put it in the woman's hand. She examined the coin, smiling as she dropped it into her apron pocket. Reuben asked, "I was to meet some friends here, don't know if they've been here yet. Two wagons, one with canvas top, a

Parson, woman and her son, and a family of coloreds. Have they been through?"

The woman smiled her almost toothless smile, nodded, "Just this mornin'. The Parson said to tell you, if ye be Reuben, they'd be in the town yonder. They was gonna be havin' a meal an' gettin' supplies. If'n you did'n catch up to 'em, they'd leave word at the livery." She cackled as she finished, "The Parson said you'd give me an extry two bits fer that message!" and cackled again, holding out her hand.

Reuben chuckled, dug into his pocket for a quarter and placed it in the woman's hand with a "Thank you, Ma'am." She nodded, pocketed the coin and watched as Reuben turned back to the door. She followed him out onto the porch, went to a bell hanging on the porch post and rung it twice. She watched as the snoozing man at the tree rose from his nap, stretched, and walked to the ferry, waving to Reuben and Appanoose to join him. As they loaded the horses aboard, the ferryman, who appeared to be in his upper forties, well-muscled and tanned, his homespun woolen britches failing to reach his ankles or callused bare feet, a homespun shirt that fought at his braces, yet hung open to show a hairy chest that rivaled that of a bear, paid them little attention but went about his task, never speaking to the men until Reuben asked, "Had any trouble with Bushwhackers or such like?"

The man frowned as he looked up at Reuben, "What do you know about Bushwhackers?" he growled.

"Run into a few comin' across Iowa."

"What happened?" he asked, still frowning, glancing from Reuben to Appanoose.

"Last I seen of what was left of 'em, they were high-tailin' it across the Missouri border."

The man slowly nodded, his squinted eyes looking Reuben over, "Good! Ain't seen none of 'em this far north, don't cotton to." He turned his back to Reuben to return to his work but Reuben saw the man shaking his head and heard him mumble something about 'trouble-makers.' When the ferry grounded, the ferryman jumped to the shore to tie the flatbed craft off, lowered the planks and motioned to Reuben and Appanoose to disembark. With no further exchange between the ferryman and Reuben, the men mounted their horses and started for the settlement of Plattsmouth.

It was a bustling town, new construction showing along the main roadway that was sided by several busi-nesses and offices. Reuben and Appanoose were side by side as they wended their way among the buggies, wagons, and horsemen that crowded the street. The boardwalks were not as crowded as the street but there were plenty of folks about. One lazy lop-eared dog lifted one eye at the passersby, and disinterested, dozed back off until the squeal of a roving pig brought him wide awake. The big dog loped off the boardwalk in pursuit of the squealer and both disappeared between the land office and Queenie's Tavern.

The livery stable was set back from the other busi-nesses and the town water trough sat at the corral fence at the side of the livery. They drew up at the trough, stepped down and let the horses have a drink as they stood looking around at the town. Across the street from the livery, the town's only two-story building boasted a sign, *Plattsmouth Hotel,* but the big windows also were lettered with *Territorial Restaurant.* Reuben looked at Appanoose, "How 'bout we go over there and have a meal?"

Appanoose looked at the restaurant and back to

Reuben, "I should keep moving. There is daylight left and I have far to go." He handed the halter lead to Reuben and reached for the blanket on the sorrel's back.

Reuben frowned, "I would give you that sorrel but he's not mine to give, but I would like to help you. We'll be going due west from here and you're welcome to ride with us Appanoose. Might save you some walking."

"I must go south," he pointed across the street that ran east/west. He turned to Reuben, extended his hand and the two clasped hands, drew one another close, and stepped apart. "You have been a friend. Perhaps we will see one another again. May the great Creator guide you as you go into the far land."

"And you, as well, Appanoose," replied Reuben as he watched his friend turn and walk down the boardwalk toward the edge of town, his blanket around his shoulders. He saw several people give the old man a wide berth, some talking to one another after they passed. Reuben started to turn away but movement caught his eye and he turned back to see two men shove Appanoose off the boardwalk and stand together, pointing at the man as he stumbled to catch his balance, and laughing. Reuben shook his head and started after his friend, who had stopped and looked back at the two ruffians. They started to move off the boardwalk but Reuben shouted, "You two! Back off!" as he stomped toward them, anger blazing from his eyes. Several others on the walk stopped to stare, knowing something was about to happen.

"Who're you to tell us what to do?" demanded the larger of the two. They were the typical town bullies, one big enough to hoist a full whiskey keg over his shoulder, the other smaller, but just as deadly as he reached to the knife at his belt.

"That man is my friend, a chief of the Meskwaki people, and should be respected as such!" declared Reuben as he drew close.

"Ain't no injun gettin' respect 'roundchere!" growled the big man, turning to face Reuben, "An' you ain't gettin' any neither, injun lover!"

Reuben motioned for Appanoose to keep moving then glared at the big man, who laughed at him, "Lookee this'n, thinks he's sumpin', tryin' to tell us decent folks what we should be doin' with them dirty injuns!" He was shouting his taunt, hoping to draw a crowd, for bullies always favor doing their deeds before a crowd to show everyone how tough they are, giving others a display of their prowess that would benefit their status among the crowds.

The man dropped into a slight crouch, hands spread wide, as he gave Reuben the 'come-on' with his fingers curling and his lip snarling. "Come on, injun lover, show me what'chu got!"

The man feinted but Reuben did not move as he watched the man draw close. Reuben had surveyed where he was, the wide boardwalk in front of a tavern that had people gathering at the window and entry. The locals knew Demas Martin was up to his usual ways and was egging on another fight. They were heard making bets on the outcome as money changed hands and shouts of encouragement were heard from the tavern patrons.

The big man laughed, looked away, and started his bull charge at Reuben. But Reuben quickly sidestepped off the boardwalk, leaping toward the hitchrail and as he moved he drew his pistol, smashing it down on the back of the head of the charging man, knocking him unconscious. The man fell to his face and skidded on the boardwalk, to come to a stop, face to face with the lazy blood hound that had returned to his napping spot.

Reuben dropped to the ground, holstered his pistol, and waved to Appanoose as he turned back to the livery. Everyone that stood near the fracas had stopped and stared at what happened and as Reuben walked away, they seemed to come awake and started jabbering and pointing, most laughing at the coldcocked bully lying in a heap. His friend had knelt by his side, trying to revive him but was unsuccessful in his attempt. With a glance to the disappearing back of Reuben, the man looked at his unconscious friend, stood and walked away.

Reuben walked into the big door of the livery, following the sounds of the smithy, and approached a big man with more hair on his arms than most men had on their heads, and as he paused, Reuben spoke, "Howdy!"

The man looked up, nodded, and continued hammering at the hot horseshoe until satisfied, then dipped it in the water, looked back at Reuben, "What'chu need?"

"Had some friends pass through, said they'd leave a message with the livery. Two wagons, one with hoops and canvas, the other'n without. Two families, a Parson, and kids. See anyone like that?"

"Was one o' the wagons carryin' coloreds?"

"That's right."

"I tol' 'em to keep goin'. We didn't need more Negras in this town. Weren't more'n a couple hours ago. Prob'ly catch 'em easy. They took the road west," growled the man, glaring at Reuben as he slowly shook his head.

Reuben nodded, "Thanks," and turned away. The horses stood near the water trough, ground tied, and the roan perked up when Reuben came from the livery. He smiled at the expectant roan, mumbling, "Why can't people be more like horses."

"**R**euben! Look Ma! It's Reuben!" shouted little Charlie as he broke away from the play he and the two Carpenter brothers were enjoying. The three stood and watched as Reuben rode into their camp, riding a different horse and trailing the familiar little sorrel. Claire stepped from the side of the wagon, an apron showing flour dust and more on her hands and cheek. She pushed back a lock of hair with her floury hand, smiling broadly at Reuben. Behind her came the Parson, smiling just as broadly as they showed their joy at the return of their friend.

It was the deep bass voice of Eli that grabbed Reuben's attention as the man walked close, "Welcome back Reuben, we've been prayin' for you right regular, and it's mighty good to see you safe n' sound." He reached up to take the lead of the sorrel as Reuben swung a leg over the rump of Blue to step to the ground. Eli continued, "Met some more folks that might be wantin' to travel with us," he spoke softly so only Reuben could hear, "Not too sure 'bout 'em, though." Eli started to the edge of the trees that hid a little creek and spoke over his shoulder to Reuben, "C'mon wit' your horse, there's water here for 'em."

Before he took a step, Claire was near, "It's so good to see you. I, uh, we were worried about you," she declared glancing to the Parson who stood near the wagon, smiling at the return of the prodigal. He nodded to Reuben and turned back to step behind the wagon.

Reuben looked up at Claire, "Tweren't much of nothin', although the bunch did hit some more farms." He frowned as he looked around, "Where's the fella from that other farm that was bein' tended to?"

"Oh, his neighbor, a sweet widow lady, had come down the road seein' the smoke, saw us tending the young man and demanded we take him to her farm that neighbored theirs, so he was happy 'bout that and we did as she bid."

Reuben nodded, understanding, and started to follow Eli as he explained, "I brought your horse back, Eli has him at the creek. Picked Ol' Blue up at one o' those little towns so I won't have to use yours."

Claire touched Reuben's arm lightly and started walking alongside as he led Blue to the water, "There's something else."

"Oh, you mean about the other wagon?"

"Well, yes, but that's not what I meant," she looked around to see if anyone was nearby, but the children had resumed their play and the newcomers were busy at their wagon and the Parson had returned to Claire's wagon. She looked at Reuben as he stripped the saddle from the roan and stepped back to let him roll. When the big horse stood, he went to the creek beside the sorrel and Claire said, "While you were gone, the Parson and I have spent most of the time together, he's been helping

217

drive my wagon and harness the mules and such, he's been a big help."

"Great, I'm glad he was here for you," replied Reuben, watching the horses start to graze.

"But," she paused, looking at Reuben, "we've, well, we've grown close," she stammered, dropping her eyes, then glancing up at Reuben.

Reuben chuckled, "That's great, Claire. I'm happy for you; you deserve a good man."

"You're not upset?"

"Upset? Of course not. Like I said, I'm happy for you."

She breathed a deep sigh, "I was so worried. I thought you would be hurt."

"Hurt? Of course not," answered Reuben, turning to face Claire. "I never thought there was anything like that between us, Claire. I was just concerned for you and wanted you to be safe. The whole idea of you going to Fort Kearny was your father's idea, and yours, of course. But after what happened, I just, well, I guess I felt a little responsible for you. You had no one to help and I was planning on going west anyway, so . . ." he lifted his eyebrows, shrugged, and smiled. "So, does this mean you're going to be gettin' hitched?"

Claire blushed, ducked her head, "We haven't really discussed marriage yet."

"Well, if he's smart, he'll hogtie you right quick 'fore you get out there with all them soldier boys and lonely farmers."

She laughed and playfully slapped him on the shoulder, causing him to wince and frown. He grabbed his arm, held it close to his side, and breathed easy, slowly relaxing.

Claire showed alarm, "What is it? Are you hurt?"

"Took a bullet a couple days ago, prob'ly need to change the bandage on it, that's all."

"Well, you get right on over to that wagon, mister, and let me tend to you proper!" she demanded. She looked at Eli who stood by the sorrel, "Eli, could you tend to both horses, take care of Reuben's gear? I have to tend to his bullet wound!"

"Yes ma'am, will do! Did you say, 'bullet wound'?" he asked, frowning.

"Yes! He was shot and needs his bandage changed."

"Then you take good care of our boy, Miss Claire. I'll tend the horses."

"Thank you, Eli," she answered as she took Reuben's hand and pulled him toward the wagon. They passed the wagon of the new family, and Claire spoke quickly, "Cathy, Richard, this is Reuben, the man we spoke about, but I must tend his wound first. We'll be back and talk soon." The couple frowned and nodded as Claire continued towing a chuckling Reuben to her wagon, without pausing to talk to the newcomers.

As she made him sit on a big rock between the wagon and the cookfire, she went to the wagon to fetch her kit of necessities and as she returned, she saw the Parson, "Peter, could you fetch us some fresh water, please. I must tend this man's wound."

"Sure, sure," he answered, snatching up the wooden bucket and starting for the creek.

"Now, Mr. Reuben," she began sternly, "Where is this wound?"

Reuben chuckled as he untucked his shirt and lifted it over his head. The bandage showed blood and Claire began unwinding the long bandage the doctor had applied with a wrap around his entire middle. As she finished with the wrap, she very tenderly started to peel the pad off the wound, both front and back, but the dried blood made it difficult to remove.

A voice came from behind her, "Perhaps if we soak it first, it'll come off easier." It was the Parson who stood with the bucket in hand, behind Claire.

She glanced up, grabbed a washcloth and was soon soaking both bandages. Once the bandages gave way, she removed them and gasped when she saw the ragged-edged wound at his back and the smoother round wound on his side. "Oh my!" but without pause, continued to wash, and cleanse the wound. She reached into her kit and pulled out a little tin of her mother's home remedy salve to apply to the new bandage.

"What's that?" asked Reuben, frowning,

"My mother's recipe, it's very good. It has beeswax, honey, plantain, rosemary, and something else. She used it on us all the time!" she declared, continuing with her work.

Within a short while, she sat back, observing her handiwork, and looked sternly at Reuben, "Now, that's healing. But you still must take care and try not to break it open again! Understand?"

"Yes, mama," replied Reuben with his best tone and expression of contriteness.

She huffed, "Oh you!" and stood with both hands on her hips, then motioned him to get up. Once he was on his feet, she stepped close and hugged him tightly. "It really is good to have you back." She stepped back, nodded, "Now, let's go meet the Walters."

The Walters were from Glenwood, Iowa, and were also bound for Fort Kearny. They had a general store in their hometown but the town was no longer prosperous, and they were looking for a new start in a new location. Richard Walters looked more like a blacksmith than a storekeeper and, what he lacked in personality, Catherine made up for with her ebullience. Their son, Richard Junior, or Ricky, was fourteen and trying hard to be a man, while their daughter, Mary Beth, sought only to emulate her mother. Both bore long curly blonde hair, usually hanging in ringlets, and the freckles across the bridge of their noses were the only smudge on their self-perceived beauty.

"Cathy, Richard, this is Reuben Grundy, our very special friend and leader of our little group," began Claire, nodding and pointing as she spoke. She turned to Reuben, "Reuben, this is the Walters family, Cathy, Richard, Ricky and Mary Beth."

Reuben nodded to each one as Claire pointed them out, "Pleased to meet you folks," he replied, offering his hand to Richard who slowly stood, giving a sidelong and obviously critical glance to Reuben.

He shook Reuben's hand, and asked, "Leader huh? You don't look old enough to lead a horse to water."

Reuben and the others were a little taken aback by Richard's remark but Reuben looked up at the man who stood both taller and wider and answered, "Leader only by their decision." He stepped back, smiled at Cathy and Mary Beth, "If you'll excuse me, I need to tend to some animals," and with a tip of his hat, he walked away from the group.

Cathy looked at her husband, "That was uncalled for Richard," she admonished, looking sternly at the man.

"He ain't nothin' but a pup! Why should we follow him anywhere? Prob'ly just get himself and ever'body else lost!" he grumbled, watching Reuben's back as he walked away, but speaking loudly enough so Reuben could probably hear.

Claire cleared her voice and both Cathy and Richard

turned to look at her, "Reuben saved me and my child from a band of murderers and raiders. He volunteered to see me and little Charlie safely to Fort Kearny. He had no obligation to do so but being the man he is, he volunteered. He also single-handedly ended the rampage of those brigands, and further, when more raiders hit other farms and killed innocent people, it was Reuben who went after them, killing most of them and saving countless lives. We will follow him no matter where he leads for I know we will always be safe with him. But, Mr. Walters, I do not recall anyone inviting you to join us and our leader as we go to Fort Kearny!" She spat the words, each one dripping with venom and correction, defending the man who was a protector to them all and attacked by a man that had yet to prove he was even that, a man! She turned on her heels and stomped away, fuming with anger.

"Now you've done it, again!" spewed Cathy Walters, sneering at her husband. "You just can't help it, can you? Always talking without thinking! Now what are we going to do?" she demanded, sitting with arms crossed over her chest, glaring at her husband.

Richard shook his head as he picked up a stick and tossed it into the fire. "I never wanted to make this trip anyway," he mumbled as he reached for another stick. "I'll talk to 'em, maybe apologize, maybe they'll take us on."

"I didn't want to make this trip either but, as I recollect, it was your doin' that got us into the mess that lost us our store!"

"Yeah, yeah, I know. How many times do I have to say I'm sorry?" he pleaded.

"Action speaks louder than words, Richard," answered Cathy, her tone ending the conversation. She rose and went to the back of the wagon to fetch the makings for their supper.

Richard stood and walked away, going to the creek where Reuben and Eli were grooming the horses. When he came near, he went to the side of the blue roan opposite Reuben and looking over the back of the horse, he began, "I said some stuff back there I'm pretty sure you heard," and was interrupted by Reuben.

"I heard. But the way I see it, every man is entitled to his own opinion," said Reuben, stroking the back of the roan with his handful of dry grass. The horse was stretching out, enjoying the attention, and Reuben kept it up, grinning at the action of the horse.

Richard continued, "It's not that. I have a bad habit of opening my mouth when it'd be better shut and that was one of those times. I guess I was just surprised at how young you appear to be and I reckon I expected some old trail hand with whiskers and such. But for what it's worth, I apologize for sayin' what I did," and extended his hand over the back of the roan.

Reuben looked at the man, nodded, and accepted the offered hand and shook it as he added, "As far as getting anybody lost, I've never been over this trail, but I've asked around a lot and most all these trails join up near Fort Kearny. Seems these were all feeder routes of the Oregon Trail that many a wagon has crossed. And as far as gettin' lost, the Parson has assured me that I can't get lost cuz I've accepted Christ as my Savior and I'm heaven bound! And although I've done some mighty bad things cuz o' this war, he has assured me I'm still goin' up when I die. Now, if you mean finding ourselves somewhere where we don't know where we are, that is entirely possible, because most folks even if they know where they are find themselves lost as a Christmas goose and couldn't find their way out of an open barn. So, best I can say is, wherever we go, we'll be goin' together. And if that's good enough for you, then you're welcome to come along."

Richard chuckled, shaking his head, and answered, "Sounds fine to me and I'm sure the missus will agree. Thanks Reuben."

Reuben nodded and returned to the task of rubbing down the blue road in anticipation of a long day tomorrow.

"Now folks, the way I figger it is we've got about a week's travel left 'fore we get to Kearny. I've talked to everyone I run into 'bout this journey and this is how it shapes up." He had a stick in hand, dropped to one knee, smoothed out the dirt and began to draw. "This here's the Missouri," making a wiggly line from the top to the bottom of his dirt map, "and here's where the Platte joins. We're here, outside of Plattsmouth and the Platte makes a big hump to the north from here," as he added the line for the Platte River, extending it far to his right in more of a straight line. "We'll head due west and tomorrow afternoon we'll pass south of Ashland, which is probably the last sign of civilization we'll see till we get to Kearny. There's an Oxbow Trail that's south of here and this one might join it but we don't know that. So from Ashland, we'll keep west until we cross the Blue River that runs north to south and that'll prob'ly be late the third day. We keep west till we hit the Platte that has turned south and west, then follow it to Fort Kearny."

He stood, looking around at everyone who looked at his crude map and up at him. "Any questions?"

"Yeah," started Richard, "Do you expect any trouble along the way?"

Reuben dropped his gaze as he chuckled a little, "I always expect trouble. I'd rather be disappointed when it doesn't come than be surprised when it does. But there is a possibility of Red Legs from Kansas comin' north and Pawnee Indians just about anywhere along the way."

Richard frowned, "Red Legs? Why would they bother us?"

"There are a lot of men that don't much care who we are or what we believe, they're just out to kill and steal whatever they can get away with, some mask themselves as Red Legs, the anti-slavery crowd, and hit any likely target, regardless of what they believe. Others, as we've seen, call themselves Bushwhackers out of Missouri, the pro-slavery bunch, and they do the same thing, all in the name of helping the war. But the Pawnee, from what I hear, anything can happen."

"So the only safe place would have been for us to stay home?" asked Cathy Walters, visibly upset.

Claire stepped forward, "Even home is not safe nowadays, Cathy."

Everyone grew silent until Reuben said, "Then let's turn in and get an early start. We still have a long way to go." He looked up at Richard and motioned him to stay. When the others had gone, Reuben asked Richard, "Do you have any weapons, you know, rifles and such?"

"I have a Colt revolving shotgun, a Spencer rifle, and a Colt Paterson pistol. I also have a Springfield muzzle-loader for my son."

"Does your wife shoot?"

"No, but I have taught her how to load all my weapons."

"Good. I just wanted to be sure and to know

everyone was ready, if need be, although I'm hoping the only thing we'll be shooting is game," replied Reuben, starting to turn away.

"About that, would it be possible for me and my son to accompany you on a scout to get in some fresh meat soon?"

"Of course. Anytime. You have saddle horses?"

"Yes, we have two horses, besides the double team we have for the wagon."

"Then we'll count on a joint scout soon. The Parson and I will take the first one but perhaps the next day."

"I'd like that, and we could use some fresh meat. Salt pork and beans can get mighty tiresome," replied Richard, nodding as he turned back to his wagon.

———

IT WAS AN EARLY START; THE THREE WAGONS WERE ON THE trail while the lowering half-moon was resting on the tree tops in the west. But that was to become the norm for the travelers, with the morning showing frost on the ground and grass nearby, the air cool with a nip that made everyone tuck their chins in their collars, and the frost showing at the nostrils of the animals. Winter was on its way and there was nothing to do but keep moving.

The third evening saw them on the bank of the Blue River, ready and willing to cross, but with the sun showing gold across the western horizon, they chose to wait till morning and make the crossing. The trees were thick on the eastern bank but the route they followed was a well-worn trail and the crossing appeared to be shallow and gravelly. The three days with three wagons had proved uneventful and late the second day, Ricky and his Pa had bagged a spritely white tail deer for the pot and both were happy. When Reuben gathered the folks together, he began to tell the result of his day's scout. "I came across sign of buffalo. Looks like a big herd and we'll prob'ly meet up with 'em tomorrow, maybe 'round mid-day."

"That sounds good! From what I hear, buffalo meat is mighty tasty!" declared Richard, glancing from one to the other. "We got that white tail easy enough, so we should be able to get us a buffalo too!"

The others nodded and mumbled their agreement, all looking forward to some different fare. But when they looked at Reuben's expression, they stopped their jabber and Claire asked, "There's something else, isn't there?"

"Ummhumm. I also saw sign of a bunch of riders and I think they were Pawnee."

"Pawnee? Were they huntin' meat or people?" asked Eli, pulling Martha close.

"No way of knowing, Eli. But I'm thinkin' they were trailin' the buffalo. But I'd just as soon we don't go shootin' any buffalo until we know where the Pawnee are and what they're up to, at least for a while."

"Sounds reasonable to me," spoke up the Parson. "No reason why we can't do without buffalo meat for a few more days, we're well supplied."

"Then everybody check your weapons, make sure they're clean and loaded and that everybody knows how to use them. Keep them handy and don't hesitate when necessary but don't go shooting unless I give you the go-ahead." By the time everyone turned in, all the weapons had been cleaned and reloaded and placed near at hand.

They felt it before they heard it but the sound soon brought them wide awake. It was the rumble of thousands of hooves, the clatter of horns, the bellowing of big bulls, and the bleating of young calves, all blending together to sound like the low rolling thunder of a mid-summer storm. Reuben was the first to rise and search their surroundings for what he immediately knew was the buffalo herd. The splash of water told him they were crossing the river, but the sound was coming from upstream. He had spotted a low swale north of their camp and reckoned that to be the chosen crossing of the herd. Although the river was forty feet across and as deep as the belly of a horse, it did little to slow down the migrating herd. It was late fall, early winter, and the bison usually made their way to the southern climes to spend the winter and would probably move further south from here.

The big moon, although only about a half-moon, gave ample light on this clear night to see the rolling mass of bison. The camp of the travelers was on a slight rise to the east side of the river and was just high enough to give a good view of the passing herd as they moved into a wide flat with tall grass. Reuben noticed the lead bulls were slowing and starting to graze, prompting the entire herd to begin milling and grazing. The big flat offered ample grass, even for a herd this size, at least for several days. He grinned as he realized they were near enough for them to ride close and maybe kill one or two for their larder. He knew these beasts were huge and the meat would be more than ample for the entire group, and then he thought of the Pawnee. If the buffalo were near, the Pawnee would be also, and that might present a problem.

The entire group was gathered around the campfire, the sun yet to rise but was taunting them with the thin grey line above the eastern horizon. "So, we goin' after some buffalo this morning?" asked Richard, not really asking permission but trying to determine what Reuben was thinking.

"I think it would be best to find the Pawnee. If we were to go shooting into that herd and maybe spook them the wrong way, who knows what damage they would cause. And if the Pawnee are planning a hunt and we do something that interferes with that, they might not be too happy with us," explained Reuben.

"Who cares about a bunch of Indians? Besides, there's plenty of buffalo for ever'body, isn't there?" retorted Richard.

"Just how many to you plan to kill?" asked Reuben.

"Well, I figger to get one and Ricky here would like to get one."

"There's enough meat on one of those bison to feed this entire bunch for a couple weeks!" declared Reuben, growing impatient with Walters.

"So. There's so many out there and that's just one herd. We could kill a dozen and let 'em lie and no harm done!" snarled Walters.

"I was always taught, *Don't kill more'n you can eat,* and I have found that to be sound advice. And as long as you're with us, you will do the same. If you kill more than one, you will skin and dress every single one and if you have to empty your wagon of all your possessions, you will take every bit of meat and hide with you and eat it till it is all gone!" ordered Reuben, eyes drawn to slits as his hand dropped to the butt of his pistol.

Cathy backhanded her husband on his shoulder, "Richard!" and waited until he looked at her, then continued, "So help me if you don't do as you're told, I will leave you here on the prairie with the bison and Pawnee! And since you bought those guns," shaking her finger at the rifle leaning on the log, "with my money, I'll take them with me and everything else we own!"

Her voice wavered from the sound of a screaming banshee to that of a raging tornado and everyone was astounded as she chastised her husband who towered over her shaking finger. He gritted his teeth as he took her scolding, shaking his head and seeming to melt before her. He didn't even glance at the others, just stood before her and took everything she dished out. When she stopped, she put her hands on her hips, and added, "Do you understand me?"

He nodded his head and sheepishly turned away from the others and walked to the wagon. The others watched, mesmerized at the power the woman had over the big man but no one dared to speak a word. She looked at them, nodded her head and slapped her hands together as she summoned her son, "Ricky! Go with your father!" and lowered her voice as her countenance changed when her daughter came near, "There, there, dear. Everything will be alright, don't you worry." She stood erect and looked at Reuben, "I'm certain you will have no more trouble from my husband, Reuben. Thank you." Before anyone could respond, she turned and walked to the wagon, her daughter at her side and under her arm.

Reuben decided to keep Walters close and suggested he join him for the early morning scout. The somewhat restrained man nodded and asked, "My son?"

Reuben frowned, "Just us for now." He stepped aboard the roan and checked both rifles as he waited for Walters. The two stepped out at a brisk pace, the sun painting the sky with pink and gold, off their right shoulder. Reuben was aiming for the slight rise that stood away from the river and would possibly offer them a view of the buffalo. With their camp in the trees, they had not seen how far the herd moved in the early morning hours and the breeze from the east did little to carry the smells or sounds of the herd their direction. The grass was tall and they moved quietly as they started up the slight rise where a pair of thick oaks spread long leafless branches like a toddler reaching for anything stable as he tottered to his mama.

As they started to crest the rise, Reuben said, "Let's step down, go to the trees."

With the bigger of the trees for cover, the men

ground tied their mounts and stood beside the gnarly trunk to look at the brown sea of buffalo before them. The tall grass was deeper than their bellies and the mass appeared as brown humps swimming in the waving grass that yielded to the east winds. Occasionally a big head would raise, his beard and nose still in the grass, and look around, then drop his head and continue. Movement in the grass showed the presence of orange-colored calves that occasionally jumped high as they romped playfully in the grassy glade. The low murmur of the bellows, grunts, and snorts was muffled in the deep brownish-green of the fall grasses, but the clatter of horns told of the steady movement of the herd.

"What'chu figger? 'Bout two, three hundred yards?" asked Walters, keeping his eyes on the herd.

Reuben knew the man was already counting on shooting one or more of the wooly beasts, but he was concerned about his marksmanship. Even though he carried a .52 caliber Spencer that was deadly out to about five hundred yards, a less than capable marksman, even at two hundred yards, would do more wounding than killing.

"Why are you here?" came a gravelly voice from behind them, startling them both. The men had moved away from their horses and had not heard anything, nor watched their horses for sign of alarm. Both Reuben and Walters turned quickly, each man reaching for the pistol at their waists, but the sight of seven mounted Native warriors stopped them.

Reuben breathed easy, slowly lowering his hand from his holstered Remington, and nodded at the warriors, looking at the leader, a big man with a stern expression, his hair hung in long braids twisted with mink tails and hanging to his knees. Two feathers dangled at the back of his head, his neck and chest decorated with bone hair-pipe necklace and breastplate. With buckskin leggings and a beaded breechcloth his only clothing, the stoic expression of the man showed a foreboding air that the man was not just a leader but would be a deadly adversary. A quick glance at the others showed all were armed, with only four carrying muzzle-loading flintlock rifles, the others with lances, war clubs, and bows and arrows.

Reuben looked back at the leader, and using sign language with his spoken English, he answered, "I am Reuben Grundy, and this is Richard Walters; we're with the wagons camped yonder in the trees and were considering taking a buffalo for meat."

"White eyes kill many, waste meat!" growled the man.

"No, we only take what we can eat," answered Reuben. "Are the Pawnee after the buffalo also?"

"I am Big Spotted Horse, of the Pitahawirata band of the Pawnee people. These are Little Sun and Moon Eagle," nodding to the men on either side. "This is our herd of buffalo and we will hunt them this day."

"I see you have some rifles but not all. We could help, we have far shooting rifles and could take them from here."

Big Spotted Horse frowned, lifted a leg over the neck of his horse and slid to the ground to walk closer to Reuben. "Where are these rifles?"

"We have them but, if we use them to kill buffalo for you and your people, we will take one for ourselves, agreed?"

"We could just take the rifles from you and shoot them ourselves," growled the chief, crossing his arms over his chest, and stepping closer to Reuben.

Reuben grinned, casually stepped to the side, out of the line of sight of the other warriors and looked up at the chief who was a few inches taller and considerably broader. "But you would not live to be one that uses the rifles," as he pulled his jacket aside to show the pistol in his hand pointed at the man's belly. "But we did not come to make war with the Pawnee. Let us make your hunt easy, take many buffalo for your village. Is not that why you are here, to get meat for your village for the coming winter?"

The chief grunted, nodded, and turned to his men, motioning them to the ground. With a slight nod to Walters, Reuben had Walters move closer to the horses.

"We will see this shoots far rifle," offered the chief.

Reuben went to the roan, slipped the Sharps from the scabbard, hung his possibles bag over his head and shoulder, and walked back to the big oak. Walters joined him, Spencer in hand. Reuben looked at the milling herd, glanced at Walters, "Pick your target." While the man was choosing his target, Reuben stood leaning against the left side of the oak. Walters was on the opposite side. The big trunk was about five or six feet in diameter and separated the men by a safe distance.

"I'll take that lone one to the right, he's broadside," answered Walters.

"All right, but pick another'n also, just in case they spook," suggested Reuben.

"Ready," replied an anxious Walters.

"Take it," answered Reuben.

The big Spencer bellowed and bucked, echoed by the Sharps. Reuben's rifle blasted with a louder roar and both targets were hit. Walters' bull took a step, stumbled, and fell, but Reuben's dropped as if the legs had been cut from under him. Although the bullets were the same caliber, the Sharps had a greater velocity and Reuben was a more accurate shooter. Both men quickly reloaded, Walters by jacking the lever to bring a new cartridge into the chamber, Reuben by lowering the lever to eject the spent cartridge and slip in a new cartridge, bringing the lever up and putting a cap on the nipple.

Reuben had brought the Sharps to his shoulder just as Walters fired another round, the targeted bull staggered but walked away. Walters mumbled something as he kept his eyes on the bull while he jacked another cartridge in the chamber, took aim, and fired again. The second round dropped the bull. Reuben said calmly, "Take your time," and squeezed off his second round. The Sharps spoke again, rocking Reuben back beside the trunk, and the .52 caliber projectile broke the neck of the targeted cow, dropping her instantly. Reuben spoke, "Wait," to Walters, and turned to look at Big Spotted Horse. All the warriors were excitedly talking and gesturing toward the herd and the men but Big Spotted Horse appeared unimpressed. Yet when Reuben turned, the man nodded, "It is good." He held up his hand, four fingers in the air, "This many more."

Reuben nodded, as he reloaded the Sharps, and spoke to Walters, "Take two more, but take your time." He heard a mumble from the man as he lifted the rifle for another shot. Reuben leaned against the big oak, sighted down the telescope and picked another cow, without a calf, and squeezed off his shot. Because they were a good distance from the herd, the buffalo, although showing a little skittish, moved slowly away from the downed animals, continuing their graze. When the shooters were finished, Reuben turned back to Big Spotted Horse, "Would you like to shoot one?" lifting the rifle toward the man.

Big Spotted Horse's eyes flared wide as he looked

from the rifle to Reuben, nodding and trying hard to keep from smiling, but his enthusiasm got the best of him and he stepped forward, arms outstretched. Reuben quickly explained about the telescopic sight and the double set triggers, then handed off the rifle with, "It's loaded and ready to go. Just pick your target and squeeze off the shot."

Horse took Reuben's place by the oak, lifted the rifle carefully to his shoulder and looked down the telescopic sight, jerked back and glanced to Reuben, then hugged the rifle close and looked into the scope again. The rifle moved very little and the chief squeezed off his shot. The big rifle bucked and roared and, much to his surprise, rocked the chief back. But the bullet flew true and a cow dropped as if she had been poleaxed. Horse looked at the downed cow, back to Reuben, and smiling, handed off the rifle.

Reuben grinned as he reloaded the big gun, watching Big Spotted Horse prance in front of his men, talking animatedly about his experience with the Sharps rifle. He walked back to Reuben as he slipped the rifle into the scabbard and said, "Our women will be here to dress and skin the buffalo. We will bring the meat of one to your wagons but, now, we must go to the first kill and take of the meat. Join us." It was more of a demand than a request and Reuben nodded to Walters to come along.

The group rode from the rise to the downed animals, the herd moving further away at the sight of the riders, and each man dropped to the ground. Big Spotted Horse dropped to one knee between the legs of the cow, and with his knife, slit the animal open from gullet to tail. He reached into the steaming maw, pulling out the mass of innards and clasped the big dark red liver, cutting it free from the rest. With another quick slice, the bile pooled, and Big Spotted Horse dipped the edge of the liver in the bile, stood and lifted it high to thank the Creator for the kill and took a big bite, cutting the liver before his nose, and chewed on the chunk in his mouth as he handed the liver to Reuben with a nod and gesture for him to do the same.

Reuben took a deep breath, squinted his eyes, and dipped the liver in the bile, then repeated the actions of the chief to the cheers of the warriors, then handed the liver off to Walters with a nod. Walters looked at the bloody countenance of Reuben, thought to himself that if the kid could do it, he could, and proceeded to complete the ceremony himself. The liver was quickly consumed by the rest of the warriors and Reuben and Walters mounted up to return to the wagons. The chief nodded, "We will bring the meat soon."

Reuben nodded and reined the roan around, pointing him to the trees beside the river, and Walters moved alongside. Both men rode quiet, relishing the entire experience of being with the Pawnee and learning of their ways.

The travelers were rapt as they listened to the account of the hunters and, when they told of the upcoming visit from the Pawnee, they looked from one to another as Claire asked, "Is it safe? I mean for us to have the Pawnee come into our camp. Couldn't they kill us?"

Reuben chuckled, "I'm sure there are enough of them nearby that they could attack and overwhelm us without much trouble. But I believe Big Spotted Horse is peaceful and this is a big step he's taking to come to us. His offer to allow his women to dress out our buffalo, well, we couldn't refuse."

"Will he bring his woman with him?" asked Martha, wide eyed and even fearful.

"I don't know, maybe. But I think we need to be prepared to feed them, whoever comes. So, if you ladies don't mind, perhaps you could maybe get some biscuits cooking, maybe some beans, what-have-you, anything that's good."

"Are you implying that there is anything we fix that is not good?" asked Cathy, the woman that had excoriated her husband.

But Reuben was not about to subject himself or anyone else to her wrath and he answered simply, "Cathy, I'm certain whatever you ladies fix will be absolutely delicious."

She let a slow grin split her face and laughed as she rose to go to her wagon for the makings. The other women did the same and, in short order, there were dutch ovens sitting on and covered with coals beside the fires as well as some hanging over the cookfires.

It was late afternoon when the cavalcade of Pawnee came to the camp of the travelers. The three men that led the party of hunters rode beside their women as one of the women's horses trailed a travois loaded with the meat from the buffalo. Big Spotted Horse reined up, lifting his hand beside his shoulder, palm forward as he greeted those beside the cookfires.

"Kúha?ahat!"

"Hello, and welcome," answered Reuben, standing to greet the visitors. "Step down, join us."

Three bold men, three hesitant women, slid to the ground and stood beside their horses. Reuben looked at Big Spotted Horse, and started introducing the others, the women first, then the other men and children, each stepping forward to acknowledge the introduction.

Horse spoke to his women and they turned to the travois with the meat, and he looked at the other women, "Our women will show you how we do our meat. Some will be to cook, some to smoke and make pemmican. It is good for your women to know these things."

Reuben grinned, nodded to Claire and the others to join the Pawnee women and work with the meat. As the afternoon turned to evening, the women had become fast friends. Only Horse's woman spoke English but she translated for the others and all, even Cathy, were anxious to learn the ways of the prairie people. The native women were fascinated by the dutch ovens and the cooked biscuits and cornbread prepared by the women and Claire offered one of the cast iron pots to Horse's woman, Squash Blossom, who gladly accepted what would become a prized possession.

Reuben did most of the talking with the men, inquiring about the land before them and the animals and more. Parson Page asked about their beliefs and religion but the Pawnee were not forthcoming about what they considered sacred. By the time the native women were finished with showing the others how to smoke meat and make pemmican, Big Spotted Horse motioned for the others to prepare to leave.

It was a joyous goodbye among new friends and the travelers stood near the cookfire as they watched the Pawnee people leave. Claire was the first to comment, "I never thought I would see the day when I would sit down and become friends with an Indian woman, but it was wonderful. And what they taught us, that's something I will use time and again."

"I know what you mean," added Cathy as Martha and little Mary Beth nodded their heads in agreement.

Richard Walters added, "It's strange to know them as

a people. I was taught to hate all natives, that they were heathen and murderers but I learned from these men. They are not so different from us, family men with wives and children. Do you know that Moon Eagle has five children?" He shook his head in wonderment, looking at his own son and wondering about the children of Moon Eagle.

———

FOUR MORE DAYS OF UNEVENTFUL TRAVEL AND THE SMALL wagon train sighted Fort Kearny, a collection of adobe and wood buildings surrounding a parade ground with a towering flag pole with a big flag waving in the breeze, bidding the travelers welcome. The trail they traveled, now known as the Great Platte River Road, lay between the buildings of the fort and the wide Platte River like a spent arrow, stretching into the distance further than eye could see pointing to the western horizon that began to show the shadows of approaching dusk. Reuben motioned for the wagons to pull off the road and make their familiar triangular circle for a camp. When Reuben rode near the first wagon, driven by the Parson, Claire stood, "Is this Fort Kearny?" she asked hopefully.

"Believe so, yes ma'am. I thought I'd ride in, find the best way to contact your Uncle and see what's expected of new arrivals. Since we're not planning on going further before winter, they might have some accommodations available or . . ." shrugging and grinning.

"May I go with you?" asked Claire.

"Anybody that wants to can come with me, it just didn't seem like driving the wagons into the fort was best," he responded.

When all was settled, Reuben, Claire, Parson Page,

Eli, and Richard Walters rode into the fort, searching for answers. The Post Sutler was near the corner of the parade ground surrounded by about twenty buildings and Reuben pointed as he reined his roan that direction. The sutler was more than accommodating and, in a short while, five happy and expectant travelers exited the building, mounted up and returned to their little camp in the flats.

Claire excitedly told little Charlie and Cathy, Mary Beth, and Martha, "The sutler sent word to my Uncle and thought he would come sometime tomorrow. His place isn't too far, so he should be here early!" her excitement evident as she seemed to bounce about as she talked.

"Oh, Claire, I'm so happy for you. Finally, a home with family, that's wonderful," replied Martha. "And Eli said there were cabins we could fix up and stay the winter in until we find a place of our own, or decide to go further. We could visit!" she declared, clasping Claire's hands.

"And the sutler said there is a store in town that needs a good storekeeper! The owner is wanting to go to the goldfields in Colorado and we might be able to take it over!" said Cathy, just as excited as the other two women.

Claire added, "And Parson Page is expected at the Congregational church in Kearney. The sutler said the congregation has been patiently awaiting his arrival." She dropped her eyes to hide her blush, but Cathy touched her arm, smiling and understanding.

As the women chattered, Reuben walked by, leading his roan and Claire asked, "But what about you Reuben? What are you going to do?"

Reuben chuckled as he stopped to talk, "Oh, I dunno.

I heard there's a supply train comin' through on the way to Santa Fe and they usually need muleskinners or scouts. And the stage line is lookin' for guards and drivers. I might sign on with one o' them. No hurry, if nothin' comes up, I can always find something." He rubbed his belly, "I haven't missed too many meals 'fore now, so I'll make do." He lifted his eyes to the fading dusk and the golden lances sent skyward from the hidden sun, "Lotta country to see and things to do, all I gotta do is stay out of trouble and, sometimes, that's a full-time job!"

*TAKE A LOOK AT BOOK TWO: THE
TRAIL TO RETALIATION*

BY B.N. RUNDELL

**A CAPTIVATING, VIVID WESTERN CLASSIC – FOR FANS
OF THE TRUE WILD WEST.**

It was to be no more than a wagon train going west, but when
Reuben uncovers a plot to provide a shipment of Beecher's
Bibles to the restive Oglala Sioux, he was forced to intervene.
He knew the destruction that would come at the hands of
renegade natives armed with Springfield Rifles and in good
conscience, he forced himself to try to do whatever was
necessary to prevent that from happening.

The war was waging in the east and when the usual guard of
soldiers from Fort Kearny was no longer possible, the wagons
had to travel without the safety of the troops. An appeal to the
commandant also revealed a deeper plot that would put the
innocent travelers in more danger, prompting Reuben to
change his plans and form a plot of his own.

He knew trouble often comes in threes and an angry band of
Pawnee that had been cheated by the gunrunners brought their
own trouble. And to Reuben's chagrin, the Brule Sioux and the
Arapaho could also complicate matters for the young man who
was bound for the western plains. But if the restless and
renegade natives weren't enough, a mighty pretty blue-eyed
blonde young lady set her sights on the young plainsman.

If he could see what was coming, Reuben would probably and
gladly jump into the nearest pond of quicksand and count
himself lucky.

COMING DECEMBER 2021

Born and raised in Colorado into a family of ranchers and cowboys, **B.N. Rundell** is the youngest of seven sons. Juggling bull riding, skiing, and high school, graduation was a launching pad for a hitch in the Army Paratroopers. After the army, he finished his college education in Springfield, MO, and together with his wife and growing family, entered the ministry as a Baptist preacher.

Together, B.N. and Dawn raised four girls that are now married and have made them proud grandparents. With many years as a successful pastor and educator, he retired from the ministry and followed in the footsteps of his entrepreneurial father and started a successful insurance agency, which is now in the hands of his trusted nephew. He has also been a successful audiobook narrator and has recorded many books for several award-winning authors. Now finally realizing his lifelong dream, B.N. has turned his efforts to writing a variety of books, from children's picture books and young adult adventure books, to the historical fiction and western genres which are his first love.

Printed in Great Britain
by Amazon